A wild light burned in Christian's crazed eyes...

Lines of anger were entrenched in his face. He didn't care about defeating Weston now, but he wasn't going to settle for anything less than taking the C.A.T. cop over the edge with him.

A few steps from Weston he paused and changed his stance, as though preparing himself for a kick.

"This is it, Weston. The end of the road. I die, but you die with me." Then in a mild voice he added: "When you caught up with me on that roof, I beat you with my feet. I'll beat you with my feet tonight, too."

Weston's eyes dipped to watch his feet, and that was when Christian made his move. But not with his feet. Christian launched his whole body at the detective, swinging his arm in a wide arc meant to catch Weston in the side and carry both of the men over the edge...

Books by Spike Andrews

Tower of Blood
Kidnap Hotel
Cult of the Damned

Published by
WARNER BOOKS

CALLING ALL MEN OF ACTION...

Please drop us a card with your name and address and we'll keep you up-to-date on all the great forthcoming books in our MEN OF ACTION series – you'll know in advance what is coming out so you won't miss any of these exciting adventures. We would also enjoy your comments on the books you have read. Send to: SPECIAL SALES DEPARTMENT, WARNER BOOKS, 666 FIFTH AVENUE, NEW YORK, N.Y. 10103.

**ARE THERE WARNER BOOKS
YOU WANT BUT CANNOT FIND IN YOUR LOCAL STORES?**

You can get any WARNER BOOKS title in print. Simply send title and retail price, plus 50¢ per order and 20¢ per copy to cover mailing and handling costs for each book desired. New York State and California residents add applicable sales tax. Enclose check or money order only, no cash please, to: WARNER BOOKS, P.O. BOX 690, NEW YORK, N.Y. 10019

CRISIS AVERSION TEAM
C.A.T. #3
CULT OF THE DAMNED

BY SPIKE ANDREWS

WARNER BOOKS

A Warner Communications Company

WARNER BOOKS EDITION

Copyright © 1983 by Warner Books, Inc.
All rights reserved.

Warner Books, Inc.,
666 Fifth Avenue,
New York, N.Y. 10103

 A Warner Communications Company

Printed in the United States of America

First Printing: May, 1983

10 9 8 7 6 5 4 3 2 1

CRISIS AVERSION TEAM

CULT OF THE DAMNED

1

The city was a furnace. For three weeks there hadn't been a cloud in the sky and the merciless August sun had been pounding its relentless heat across the concrete face of New York City, scorching it and its inhabitants. And there was no letup at night. After dark the city itself seemed to give off heat, the sidewalks releasing stored-up heat into weary feet, the buildings radiating warmth and confining the steamy air between their towering concrete walls, constantly pressing its heat on the citizens of the city, like a laundry mangle. And that's how people felt: mangled, oppressed, irritated. The inescapable heat melted inhibitions and civilized restraints, put tempers on edge. In this kind of weather little old ladies stiff-armed boy scouts trying to help them across streets; young housewives sharpened their knives and thought about their husband's life insurance policies; minor traffic accidents led to pitched battles between drivers; inadvertent bumps between subway passengers escalated to violent fights.

The unending heat boiled away the eons of man's

evolution into a higher life form and returned him to the jungle, where a man will do anything—just for the hell of it. On the Lower East Side, half a dozen punks got to wondering over the frailty of the human body and decided to pull an old wino apart limb by limb. Why? Just for the hell of it. A twelve-year-old kid got interested in the principle of momentum and ended up shoving a man off a subway platform in direct line with an oncoming train. Why? Just for the hell of it. A husband in Brooklyn came home from work and was met at the door by his wife's wild eyes and her gleaming butcher's knife. She chased him three blocks before neighbors subdued her. She did it just for the hell of it. That was precisely what the city was during a heat wave—*hell*—and it made you think and do things you wouldn't ordinarily dream of. This kind of weather was a cop's nightmare. And to two cops like Detectives Vince Santillo and Stewart Weston it was the worst kind of nightmare, because they were assigned to N.Y.P.D's Crisis Aversion Team— known to most cops as the police department's garbage detail because it was assigned the toughest cases on the books. And in a nightmare garbage is a lot worse than it usually is. . . .

John Thompson was working the check-in desk when the woman came into the lobby. He was thumbing through a year-old copy of *Playboy* at the time and when he looked up and saw her push through the revolving door, his first thought was that one of the *Playboy* models had just come to life off the page, thrown on a light dress, and come walking into the hotel. She looked that good. Long legs, narrow waist, firm round breasts that obviously wanted out of her confining dress. Long blond hair framed a face that could easily launch a thousand ships. It was launching John Thompson's right now.

She was a looker, all right, the kind of knockout that was not uncommon in the Chelsea Arms two decades ago, when the hotel had been in its heyday, but hadn't been seen around here lately. And she had class. She glided across the worn carpet of the lobby like a queen, but without any condescension, as though Thompson were a human being and not just another piece of furniture.

"I'm looking for a Mr. Willson, Alexander Willson," she announced.

"Yes, miss." John Thompson made an adjustment to his trousers then got to his feet and checked the register. "Room 426," he instructed. "That's on the fourth floor, front. Take the elevator up, then walk straight along the hall; it's on your left." He wanted to keep on talking, just to keep her smiling face in front of his, but there wasn't anything left to say, so he had to be content just watching her lovely rear-end swing toward the elevators and then inside. Then he went back to *Playboy* and waxed philosophical on the inability of photographs to capture the living beauty of a young woman. He also wondered who this Alexander Willson was, and if he was such a classy guy, why he didn't stay at a hotel with more class than the Chelsea Arms.

On her way to room 426, Melissa Martin was wondering the same thing. She had been a fashion model for five years now and had never met a designer or designer's representative who would have chosen the Chelsea Arms as a meeting place. Not until now, that is. But she didn't mind. When you were being selected to model the great Signon Lancia's new winter line, you didn't ask questions or quibble about meeting places. This was her chance of a lifetime and she didn't want to do or say anything to blow it.

The door to 426 was opened by a tall young man with the good looks of an Alpine ski instructor, his blond hair and mustache making him look even younger than his thirty years.

"Come on in, Melissa," he greeted her, and stepped aside as she entered.

"Everything ready?" she asked.

"Yeah. You'll love this winter line. Why don't you get out of that dress so Mr. Willson can see you in the designs?"

They were in a sitting room that last looked modern about the year movie matinées cost a quarter, and it looked as though it hadn't been cleaned or dusted since then either. The fireplace had been bricked up, the chandelier replaced by a sixty-watt bulb, and the velour drapes by chintz curtains. The room was hot. The windows were open but the only air that came in was oven-hot, and Melissa could feel the sweat running between her breasts.

And the blond man could see the sweat, running in twin streams and making the flimsy dress material stick to her breasts. He watched it unabashed, knowing that as a model, Melissa was so used to being stared at that she didn't even notice his hot eyes on her. She had long ago started to treat her body like a tool of the trade, an object that she used but was not really a part of her, the way a carpenter uses a hammer in his trade.

Melissa reached for the dress's zipper along her spine, tugged it down, and shrugged out of the dress. She tossed it across the back of an armchair, then went through the doorway on the left into a bedroom, where she expected to find Signon Lancia's latest creations lying on the bed. All she found was a tattered bedspread with the hotel's insignia fading off the front. She glanced at the closet, but the hangers were empty. Puzzled, she turned back to the blond man, her naked breasts swinging in a gentle arc.

The blond man watched her from the doorway, a smile on his thin lips, a hot light glowing deep in the blue eyes.

"Where are the clothes, Mitch?" This was answered only by a broadening of his smile, and the movement of his eyes across her body, as tangible as probing hands. "There aren't any clothes, are there, Mitch?" she demanded. "No Mr. Wilson, no Lancia originals. Just a long line of bull to get me here. And I fell for it! I was dumb enough to think that an A-one klutz like you had an in with Lancia. I must have been crazy!"

"Take off the panties, Melissa."

"Like hell I will!"

She moved to get by him, but he blocked the doorway. It wouldn't have done any good to get back into the next room anyway because her dress was gone from the chair, and she could hardly go out dressed as she was.

"Come on, Mitch, let's cut the game, the joke's over. You've had your fun."

"My fun's only beginning because the joke is just beginning. And it's all on you," he murmured.

"The panties. Off with them." She opened her mouth to protest, but froze that way when she felt the cold blade of a knife laid flatwise across her breast. "Off with them," Mitch repeated.

Eyes held by his coldly handsome face—she obeyed. She might not have been aware of her nakedness before, but she was aware of it now, and of her vulnerability. She felt a growing sickness knot her stomach but smiled with as much sincerity as she could muster and, trying to reason with him, said, "Look, Mitch, if you want—"

"Shut up and listen to me," he interrupted roughly. "You have two choices. Do what I say and maybe get some good money for it. Or not oblige me, and become a very challenging job for a plastic surgeon." He flicked the knife once under her nose to make his meaning more than clear enough, and she went still as any animal sensing danger. "What's it going to be, Melissa?"

"S–sure, Mitch. Anything you say."

He pushed her back onto the bed, and started to tie her hands to the bedposts.

"Hey, Mitch, that's not necessary. I promise I'll—"

He slapped her so hard her teeth rattled. "That's what your promises mean to me." When he'd got both wrists tied he said, "There'll be a couple of guys coming in here to, uh, visit you. They won't hurt you, they just want to get it off with a model. Be obliging, kiddo, and keep your mouth shut or . . ." He finished the sentence by slowly turning the knife blade in the hot sunlight streaming through the window, making it glint like a surgeon's scalpel under operating lights.

Then he departed with a smile that made her feel

sick, and she was certain she would throw up. She turned her head on the hard pillow, and then thought of what Mitch would do if she messed up the bed like that, and that thought calmed her. Tears streamed from her eyes without her being aware of it, and she struggled against the ropes until her wrists were raw and bleeding.

She was still struggling when the door opened and a paunchy balding man in a three-piece gray pinstripe entered the room. He watched her struggling a moment, then approached the closet, where he undressed, meticulously removing wrinkles and carefully hanging each article of clothing on a hanger before coming over to the bed. Then Melissa watched in absolute disgust and amazement as he knelt between her legs and lowered his smiling mouth to her crotch like a cow reaching down to graze in high grass. When he was finished and gone, the next man came in right away, as though he'd been impatiently awaiting his turn. He undressed quickly, his eyes never leaving Melissa. Then he crawled onto the bed and thrust himself between her spread thighs. Melissa prepared herself for a long ordeal, but this guy must have been going for some kind of speed record because no more than five seconds had passed before he was in and out and on his way back to the closet, carefully dressing himself as neatly as when he'd come in.

The next man took longer and seemed to enjoy it more. The fourth was with her for nearly an hour, but all he did was lie down next to her, curl up in a fetal ball and, rocking gently back and forth, hum a nursery song to himself. All of these men looked like business executives, like any of the dozens of men who slyly ogled her on the streets; they were not at all alarmed by her being tied up. Then a pair of guys who looked like typical street toughs came in together. They took her at the same time, with her sandwiched between themselves, and this time it was painful, but the two men didn't seem to notice: they talked to each other non-stop during the whole session, describing in detail what they each were doing and how it felt. Melissa felt like the debased receptacle for the communion between these two men: they really wanted sex with each other but couldn't face their own desire.

Melissa detached herself from the abuse her body received. She experienced it all as though it were happening to another person. Melissa—the core of her—was high up in the room looking down on an unfamiliar body that was used and abused by a procession of faceless men. She felt pity for that poor woman down there, was glad that it wasn't her down there: she had completely dissociated herself from her body, held a secret part of herself away from these men, saved and cherished it as something they could not touch.

From the next room Mitch Roundtree watched these events from a hole he had drilled in the wall that morning. He recorded the afternoon's activities in detail with a 35mm Leica camera, getting each face in excellent focus. There would be no difficulty in identifying the participants in this afternoon's games, and that meant that Roundtree could demand and get a fair amount of money. When the last man had paid Mitch for the privilege of using Melissa, he packed away his Leica, and returned to the bedroom. When Melissa saw him come in, relief flushed across her face and tears welled up in the large brown eyes. "It's over," she gasped.

"Not quite," Mitch informed her. He unzipped his pants, and now her tears flowed unabated. But no pity stirred in Mitch. He remembered a certain Saturday night a month ago when he had brought her back to his apartment and had tried to make love to her, but had been unable to get aroused and she walked out, laughing at him. That cruel laughter still rang in his ears, drowned out her sobs now, as he felt only a sharp loathing for this woman and her abrupt rejection. She was getting no less than she deserved for the way she had treated him. He would show her that he was not an impotent weakling.

And he tried, but again his body failed him, and the failure fueled his growing anger. This had never happened before, he told himself, he'd been successful with every woman he'd met—until he'd met Melissa. She was to blame, this teasing bitch who waggled her ass at him, and then—somehow—made sure he couldn't do anything about it. If this bitch weren't around he'd never have any trouble... he pulled out the knife.

"Mitch—what are you doing with that knife—take it easy!"

"I never had this trouble before you, bitch. Never! And since you it's all I've had." He scraped the ball of his thumb slowly across the blade edge, smiling at the feel of its cold sharpness.

"Now, Mitch, you know that's not true."

"So you've talked to the others, eh?"

"Uh, no, I—Mitch, it's not me that does this to you. It's—it's the heat. That's it, it's the heat. The heat, Mitch, it takes it out of you. Casanova himself couldn't get it up in this weather. Wait till the heat lets up and you'll be back to normal—"

The knife went in easily, smoothly and surely, the way he had wanted to enter her some minutes ago. He opened up her throat with the blade. All he could think of, filling his mind like the blinding August sun was his failure, and his frantic hands did their work almost without his awareness. When he was finished with her he was covered with his sweat and spattered with her blood.

She was right. It was hot, the hottest Mitch had ever known—the heat fogged the mind, blurring thoughts. It took it out of you, all right. Mitch felt as weak and drained as if it were his blood that stained the white sheets. He got to his feet, taking a few minutes to compose himself, then took a long cold shower that helped clear the hot fog in his head. He took his time dressing and then he left the room. At the doorway he turned and looked back at the body that had once been Melissa—a slow smile came to his lips—and he laughed gently to himself. He was still laughing softly minutes later when he walked past John Thompson in the lobby and out into the oppressive sunshine of New York City.

Three hours later, at seven fifteen in the evening, the city was still cooking, as though the full moon that now hung in the twilight sky gave off as much heat as the setting sun. Near Times Square, there was some relief from the sun in the long shadows of the buildings, but there was no escaping the merciless breeze that all day long had blown hot as a blast from a furnace down the concrete and steel canyons of the city. It seemed to bore right into a man's body, burning him dry as desert sand on the inside, leaving him a weak shell of a man.

That was how the men and women looked to Abdul Abidi, and he was able to observe them with an objective eye because he was comfortably ensconced in the rear seat of his air-conditioned Cadillac limousine. He had been scrutinizing the passersby on Eighth Avenue rather carefully, since it was from among these women that he expected to select the three that would give him sexual pleasure tonight.

"That one"—Abdul Abidi pointed to a tall blond in spike heels, and the driver pulled to the curb. Abidi's bodyguard got out of the front seat and approached the woman.

"Excuse me, madam," he said in a rich baritone. "My name is Farah, and I was wondering if I could take just a couple minutes of your time." Farah took the surprised but curious woman by the arm, and gently led her across to the open rear door of the limousine, where Abdul Abidi's lean form was framed in the cool interior.

"This is the revered hakim Abdul Abidi"—Farah introduced his country's leader.

"I saw your picture in the paper," the woman said with awe. "You're from Egypt..."

"He is the head of state of Sabindi," Farah corrected. "The third largest diamond producing country in the world."

The woman did the appropriate oh-ing and ah-ing

and said how honored she felt to meet them, but that she could not imagine why they'd stopped to talk to her.

"The revered hakim would like the honor of your company at dinner tonight. At his Hilton presidential suite."

"You're joking! What's the catch?"

"There is none, I assure. Just an evening's entertainment that will be to both of your liking. Our driver will escort you home in the morning."

"In the *morning*. I'll have you know I'm a married woman."

"Ah, excuse me, madam. In that case our driver will escort you home tonight." The woman just stared, open-mouthed in surprise, as Farah took a velvet string purse from his coat pocket and opened it on his large palm. Three small diamonds glinted in the folds of black cloth. "The selection of an appropriate reward will be yours, madam." She hesitated, a glint in her eye that perfectly mirrored the glint of the diamonds in his palm, and Farah knew the battle was all but won. He murmured, "Why don't you think it over in more comfort, madam?" and he ushered her into the back seat of the limo where Mozart swirled in the cool air and ice swirled in vintage cognac.

Married women, Farah reflected with a smile, were the easiest to net. They were much more flattered by the attention than were single women, and more eager for some kind of escape from the boredom of their regular lives. They were also easily persuaded by diamonds. And weeks later, when they discovered that the stones they'd been given were nothing more than excellent paste imitations, to whom could they protest? Their husbands would not be terribly sympathetic. Yes, married women were the best.

Farah got back into the car and the limo glided slowly away from the curb down Eighth Avenue, its owner occasionally peeking out from behind the black curtain he'd drawn across the windows, the woman's doubts already beginning to dissolve in chilled cognac and warm compliments.

The slow progression of the limo down Eighth Avenue was noted by very few people that evening, least of all by the man looking out the hotel window at the windows of the building across the street. As he gazed at the windows, his hands were busy assembling a high-powered rifle.

He was feeling the heat. Sweat rolled in large drops off his furrowed brow, stinging his eyes. He cleared his eyes with a gloved palm, then went back to the task of assembling the rifle. When the rifle was whole, he attached a silencer to the end of the barrel, made a couple of minor adjustments to the telescopic sights, then lifted the gun and cradled the stock butt against his muscular shoulder. It was like the firm caress of a loving hand against him. He looked along the smooth barrel.

The powerful sights pulled him right across the street and plumped him down in the room across the street, where an old timer with a three-day beard on his haggard face was sipping beer in front of a television set with a fan propped up on it. The sniper sights moved to the next window where a woman in a slip was ironing a dress. One floor down, a prostitute was tucking a couple of bills into her purse and getting ready to put on a strip show for the three laughing sailors sitting on the bed.

The armpit of the city, the sniper thought, a cesspool that needs cleaning up before it spreads its filth all across the land.

He laid the cross hairs on the prostitute's back to see if it felt right. It did—the cross nestled like a blessing between her bare shoulders—and he knew she would be one of today's targets.

The sniper moved the sights to other windows: a dark room with the television playing to an empty couch; a couple of old women naked as the day they were born, sitting at a table and playing mahjong, fanning themselves and swilling beer from cans like a pair of thirsty truckers. And then he came to a room with a man in a shabby business suit sitting on a bed and a woman kneeling down in front of him. His fingers were twined in her hair, guiding her head between his legs. The sniper had seen the woman on the street a couple of minutes ago.

He looked back to the street where he saw prostitutes, waiting in pairs in doorways between magazine shops and skin flick houses, swinging their hips along the crowded sidewalk as they eyed the passersby and the drivers of cars that would pull over to get the going price. One of these women was stark naked under her loose-fitting raincoat. Every once in a while she would give a prospective customer a sneak preview by flashing open the coat. She flashed once for a husband and wife who happened to be walking by, and that couple walked for a full block glassy-eyed and red with embarrassment.

The sniper kept on choosing his targets: the stripper and the other one in the rooms; three from the street; the raincoat, one standing in a doorway, and another, a redhead slowly pacing the block. He removed the scope from his eye and just looked out at the teeming kaleidoscope of the city; the blinking neon, and flashing storefronts, headlights and taillights and stoplights, the crazy parade of rainbow colors worn by pimps, hookers, and johns, the winos and shills and con-men and junkies, and the decent hard-working citizens on their way home or to the theatres. And as the sniper looked, his five targets stood out from the confusion as if they glowed with a radiation that only he could detect. They were destined for his long gun, he could feel it, and that was good. In the shifting welter of bodies below, these five were like stones of a single color in a kaleidoscope, unified by their color, by their common destiny.

He brought the rifle up, and then suddenly became aware that the Caddy limousine that had been coming slowly down the street now pulled to the curb. A man got out of the front seat and went over to talk to the redhead. It would spoil the sniper's pattern if one of the selected victims was to get away, so he swung the rifle down and put her in the cross hairs. His fingers squeezed with the gentle yet firm movement of a natural marksman, and the rifle bucked once, its barrel snapping upward with a lance of flame, releasing no more sound than a muffled "pfft."

For one brief moment as the rifle barrel spat flame, the sniper felt as though the black cross hairs of the scope were branded onto the redhead's sinful body. Then a red rose blossomed on her white dress and the impact of the bullet hit her like a truck, shoving her straight back into the window of a little café. She crashed through the window in a dazzling shower of glass. The man who had been talking to her—Farah—spun around, dropping to one knee, then dived for the open door of the limo, which was off and moving almost before he had finished the jump. The car moved away so suddenly that some witnesses thought that it was the murderer escaping, and the danger was over. But it was just beginning.

The sniper swung the cross hairs past the stunned faces of people on the sidewalk, and found the raincoat woman who was walking swiftly away from the direction of the redhead's slaying. He squeezed off a shot that caught her in the temple, opened her head like a dropped melon, and a shower of blood and gray matter geysered in the artificial light. The dum-dum bullet fragmented on impact and flying pieces caught three other people who happened to be passing by on the crowded street, dropping them in unison, as if they were all part of the same injured body. In spite of this, it took a few seconds for the people on the street to tumble to what was going on because no one had seen a muzzle flash, nor heard the report of a gunshot. It was as though people were randomly succumbing to heart attacks. But then the truth seeped in and suddenly there was panic of the worst kind: people running into each other and into moving cars in a desperate attempt to escape from an unseen enemy, not knowing which place was safe and which was not.

The sniper moved to the next target, but the woman was gone from the doorway. He lowered the scope from his eye and again took in the whole street, knowing that she would leap to the eye. But she was nowhere to be seen.

An animal tension came into the sniper: he had to find her, could not break the pattern, could not leave incomplete the preordained configuration of death. Yet he could not see her among the terrified pedestrians seeking shelter. Women's screams started coming up from the street below.

With a tension that bordered on physical pain, the sniper raised the gun to the first of the two windows he'd selected. The stripper was just now pulling off her bra and dangling it in front of her audience. The slug exploded into her right side just above the breast and then erupted out the lower half of her body and she folded over like a cardboard cutout, falling into her own blood on the carpet. The sniper swug over one window and put a bullet into the other prostitute's spine. He lowered the rifle and then scanned the street again, and again was unable to locate the intended fifth victim. He would not leave until he got her, it would not be right. Sweat had soaked through his shirt and he was nearly blinded by the perspiration dripping into his eyes. He armed his forehead dry, and then he saw a light go on in one of the windows across the street, and he knew it had to be her: she'd fled the street and gone up to her apartment. An inner calm spread through him like ripples in a pond, as he brought the rifle up and pinned the lighted window with the scope, waiting for her to come and look out.

Police sirens pierced the traffic noise, but the sniper waited patiently, feeling no panic. He had work to complete before he could go.

A face appeared in the window, a pale shape that

immediately exploded like a balloon into a mass of red as the woman fell back into the room

Satisfied, the sniper calmly dismantled the rifle, wrapping each part in oilskin, then wrapping the whole in a blanket which he put into an Adidas bag. He left the room, not removing his gloves until he was in the elevator on the way down to the lobby.

As he stepped outside under the lights of the hotel marquee, a cabbie was standing by his cab and taking in the pandemonium across the street with the philosophical calm of a man who has seen everything.

"Some crazy let loose with a gun," the cabbie informed him.

"Anybody hurt?"

"Half a dozen, I'd guess."

The sniper tsk-tsked a bit, saying rhetorically, "What makes people do it?"

"I'll tell you what makes 'em do it," the cabbie announced without hesitation. "It's the heat. It bakes the brain so that a guy'll do anything, and I mean *anything*." But he broke off his discourse with a shrug when he saw the man's back receding into the darkness up Eighth Avenue, and went back to watching the scene across the street.

"Yep," he said to anybody who was around to listen, "it's the heat. The goddamn heat."

2

"I've heard a lot about you two, and I don't like one word I've heard," Captain Bracken said to Detectives Santillo and Weston. "You think you can live by your own law. Well, you can't. Not in my precinct you don't. In my precinct you better tread nice and gentle or you'll be standing the rest of the summer on the unemployment line. You understand me?"

Santillo and Weston maintained a stoical silence. They were used to being on the receiving end of this kind of lecture from a precinct commander. For one thing, everywhere they went they were preceded by their reputation for disliking the bullshit rules that often hinder a cop's work. For another, whenever they took over an investigation from other detectives, those detectives were resentful. And Captain Bracken was no exception: he didn't like having the investigation of the fashion model's murder taken out of his control and dumped in the laps of C.A.T. But most likely Captain Bracken wasn't as upset as he pretended to be: this was the third model murdered this summer, and the investigation was still on square one. He must have felt some relief that a hot potato had been taken out of his hands. Santillo and Weston were used to handling hot potatoes, and hot captains, too; so they waited patiently a bit longer, hoping that Captain Bracken would soon run out of steam.

The three of them were in the sitting room of the murder scene, and all around them, lab men were busy collecting evidence, vacuuming the floor and furniture for telltale pieces of dirt and thread, dusting everything in sight for fingerprints, measuring the distance between splotches of blood on the floor and walls.

The woman's body and all the evidence collected there would be taken to headquarters and analyzed by the state's top minds in forensic science, using the very best laboratory facilities and equipment that taxpayers' money could buy. The evidence would be collated and statistically broken down by computers as sophisticated as those at Cape Canaveral; then it would be sifted through by the best cops on the force, the best-trained, most experienced minds available anywhere in the world. And, if the past two murderers were any indication, all of this crime-solving machinery would come up with a single fact: the killer was probably a man.

Some crimes can't be solved by armchair deduction à la Sherlock Holmes; some require a couple of guys who'll go out and get their hands dirty, their noses bent poking around in places they shouldn't be poking. A couple like Santillo and Weston.

Their patience at an end, Santillo and Weston stepped around Captain Bracken and headed for the murder room. Bracken was standing there with nothing but empty air to lecture to on the discretion he required in investigating crimes in his precinct.

"Hey," protested Captain Bracken. "Where are you two going?"

"We thought we'd start investigating this murder," replied Weston. "That's what we're paid to do—not listen to lectures."

"I'm not finished with you two."

"Put the rest of the lecture on tape," suggested Weston, "and mail it to us."

The two detectives left Captain Bracken to fume by himself and they entered the murder room. It was a deceptive scene: at first glance it seemed there were two dead women in the room, one lying spread-eagle on the bed, hands tied to the bedposts; the other woman lying on the floor by the bed, a knife standing upright between her breasts. A second glance was required to recognize that the figure on the floor was not a woman but a department store mannequin. Her body and head were very realistic, especially the head... another step closer and Santillo and Weston could see that the head was in fact real: the woman on the bed had been decapitated and her head switched with the mannequin's. The once-beautiful living body was left with the stylized face of a department store dummy. It gave to an already gruesome scene an aura of madness that chilled the blood.

A police photographer who came into the room to take some photographs took one look at the body on the blood-soaked mattress, and headed out to look for a bathroom. He returned a minute later, looking green around the gills, and started taking pictures while Santillo and Weston talked to the Medical Examiner, a short wiry man in his sixties, with white hair and a goatee to match.

"She's been dead since this afternoon," the M.E. informed them. "I'd say the cause of death is obvious: people do not tend to live too long when they become detached from their heads. Everyone of this guy's crimes involve some kind of mutilation. He stabbed the first victim one-hundred and twenty times; he cut off the hands and feet of the second one. And now this. I'd hate to think of what the next poor woman will look like when he's through with her."

"What can you tell us about a loony who kills like this?" Captain Bracken asked the M.E.

Santillo murmured, "The killer doesn't like women."

"Don't get funny," Captain Bracken snapped. "I asked the doc." He looked at the little man. The M.E. thought a minute then shrugged and informed the captain: "He doesn't like women."

While Captain Bracken was getting red in the face, Santillo asked the M.E.: "Any evidence of sexual intercourse?"

"Plenty, which means this murder is different from the others."

"Different in what way?"

"There was no sign of sexual intercourse with the first two victims. That's not unusual with psychos like this one. Their impotence is usually part of the reason they kill. But now the pattern is broken: the guy must have got it off with her three or four times."

Santillo and Weston mulled that over for a while, then the latter asked: "Any chance there was more than one man involved?"

The M.E. looked startled by the suggestion, then gave it some thought, finally deciding: "That's an idea worth looking into. I can't answer definitely until I run lab tests. I'll let you know."

Santillo and Weston roamed around the room for a couple of minutes, trying to piece together the killer's movements from the pattern of smeared blood on the floor. It was difficult for them to move around without stepping into puddles of drying blood. The killer hadn't bothered stepping around them, and his bloodied tracks led across the bedroom into the bathroom where he had apparently showered. The odor of his scented soap hung heavily in the air, a distinctive smell, strong as flowers.

After a couple minutes of having Captain Bracken follow them around like a mother hen, as if he thought they were going to steal the hotel towels, Santillo and Weston went down to the lobby where they found the clerk John Thompson under the lighted marquee, holding a press conference like some politician. They hauled him back into the lobby.

"How about telling us what happened here today," Weston said. "We can't pay you as much as the press, but we'd like the truth just the same."

"They didn't pay me anything!" But his protest was belied by the clutched hand he wouldn't bring out of his pocket. If Captain Bracken had been doing his job instead of lecturing Santillo and Weston, he would have seen to it that the hotel clerk was kept away from the press until he'd been interviewed by detectives.

"Let's hear your story," Weston said.

"There's no story. She came into the hotel about one o'clock this afternoon. A real dream, she was, too." And he went on like that, decorating every sentence with the sort of flowery descriptions newspapers loved but cops knew simply hid the truth. There was no telling how much was fabricated to make the story interesting and how much was true. One fact was inescapable: so many people—both visitors and residents—had passed through the lobby in the course of the day that John Thompson had no idea whether or not he might have seen the killer among them. He had not seen the man who had rented the murder room. The room had been paid for by mail a week in advance, and the key had been delivered in an envelope to the mail desk of another hotel, where it could easily be picked up by anybody asking for the right name. This was the same m.o. the killer had used in the first two murders, only the name had changed. This time the name was Willson, which meant nothing to John Thompson and even less to Santillo and Weston.

When the two detectives had finished questioning the clerk, a couple of newspaper reporters sneaked over to them and started asking questions.

"Is this the work of the model killer?" one asked Santillo.

"Did he use a knife to mutilate the body again?" the other asked Weston.

"The Department will have a news release for you some time tonight," Santillo informed them. "Right now we'd like you to leave the premises so we can get on with the investigation."

"When will the—?"

"Who do you think—?"

"Scram," Santillo said, not loudly but firmly, and the reporters shut up and took their leave.

Santillo and Weston didn't look much alike. They

were both in their early thirties, but Weston stood six two and in denim pants and sport coat you might think he were skinny, until you got a look at his lean hard-muscled arms and chest. His hair and sideburns were long enough to annoy his police superiors. Santillo, on the other hand, stood a shade under six feet and had the muscular build of a light-heavyweight in fighting trim. His wavy black hair was the kind women liked to run their fingers through, and Santillo wasn't the kind of fellow to deny a woman's wants. His taste in clothes ran from Pierre Cardin to Christian Dior rather than Weston's Robert Hall specials. On the surface they had nothing in common, but looking at them you knew right away they were twins under the skin: they both possessed a cool confidence and an air of competence that told you there wasn't much they would shy away from. That was why the reporters quietly left without a fuss instead of pressing them for more information. But before stepping outside each reporter turned to take a quick photo of the two cops.

"Your pictures are going to be in the papers," the clerk said in awe.

"I hope they got my best side," Santillo joked.

"They couldn't have," Weston commented. "You weren't bending over at the time."

"At least my clothes won't put the Department to shame," Santillo rejoined. Tonight Santillo was immaculately dressed in gray slacks and shirt, a blue sports coat with a navy blue tie, and a pair of hand-crafted Italian shoes that must have kept some cobbler busy for six months.

Weston's only comment was: "Gray doesn't suit you."

At that moment a heavy-set man in his late forties strode into the lobby. Lieutenant John Hunt, Santillo and Weston's commanding officer at C.A.T., walked over to Santillo and Weston the way he always walked: with the steady, relentless movement of an armored tank in enemy territory. And the look on his hard face was about as friendly and inviting as a tank's.

"We've got another batch of trouble," he growled as he took the two detectives out of the clerk's hearing. "Another sniping—this one right smack dab in the heart of the city, just off Times Square. Five dead and three wounded, half a dozen injured in the panic to get off the streets. The commissioner just called and gave us the go-ahead to take over the sniping investigation along with the model murderers. The shooting in Times Square ended just minutes ago, so I want you two to get over there while it's still hot." He frowned at the last word, then pulled out a handkerchief and mopped his sweet-dewed bald pate. "Everything's hot in this damn weather, but not half as hot as these two cases. The commissioner's sitting on my ass for results. The mayor's sitting on the commissioner's. And now I'm going to be sitting on yours. I want these two cases solved—*yesterday!* Understand?"

"Sure," Weston commented sourly. "And while we're at it, we'll eliminate poverty, clean up the slums, and figure out the oil shortage. That'll still leave us free to go to the beach this weekend."

Lieutenant Hunt sighed. "I suppose you've been giving Captain Bracken that brand of talk, too. Christ, when will you two learn that a little diplomacy goes a long way."

"So does a little poison," murmured Santillo.

"Which is what you guys will be having for breakfast if you don't get two killers in the tank fast." He leveled a glance at them like a loaded gun. "You're going to have some help on these two. Detective Matt Christian joins us tomorrow. Teach him the ropes, but for God's sake, go easy. With you two that means try not to get him killed the first day on the job. Now get your butts over to Times Square. I'll clean up here for you."

The blocks north of Times Square were a mess. The scene of the sniping had been roped off and cars were being redirected around the block, causing bumper-to-bumper jams-up and leaving drivers to swelter in the heat and lean on their horns to get vengeance on the world for doing this to them. The traffic was so bad that Santillo and Weston had to double park four blocks from the scene, and go the rest of the distance on foot. The sidewalks were crowded, and near the scene people were jammed five or six deep around the cordon, trying to get a glimpse of the victims. Santillo and Weston pinned their shields to their jackets and waded into the crowds.

The clean-up operation was just beginning, and the street looked like a war zone. Half a dozen ambulances idled at the curb, their turning lights spilling red all over the streets; cops running around trying to round up witnesses and quell the hysteria of screaming women; paramedics ministering to the wounded; ambulance and morgue attendants carrying away the injured and the dead. It was an open-air madhouse and it had been created by one man with a rifle. Both cops felt the anger and outrage that all civilized men feel when confronted by the aftermath of senseless violence and death.

A tall, hard old cop with the bulging eyes and beaked nose of an eagle came up to them and told them everything was under control.

"It don't look that way, but it is," he assured them, surveying the street.

"How long ago did it happen?" Weston asked.

"Shooting stopped about twenty minutes ago."

"You found his nest yet?"

"Haven't had time."

It was important to find the sniper's nest as soon as possible. The importance of getting onto a criminal's trail before it grows cold is a well-worn cliché; but like a lot of clichés it became well-worn precisely because it was true. Santillo and Weston had once cracked a case because they had quickly managed to find the place a killer had sat in a café: they got to the table before a discarded cigarette had burned away its identifying trademark, and that distinctive trademark had nailed the guy.

A witness to the sniping was able to tell them where the redhead had been standing just before she had been shot, so the two detectives went over to the stretcher where her body lay zipped up in a body bag, and tried to determine the sniper nest's height above the street by estimating the bullet's angle of entry and exit. It was a messy job because the once-attractive body was floating in a pool of blood and viscera. And it was a difficult job because the dum-dum bullet had exploded in pieces out her back, making it nearly impossible to decide on an angle of exit. As they were doing this unpleasant work one of the prostitutes who was still standing around muttered to a friend.

"Cold-blooded bastards, those two. You can bet your ass they wouldn't poke around like that if she was one of those Park Avenue princesses instead of a pross like us."

The two cops knew how she felt, but they also knew that to get a clue to this killer they would poke around anybody, regardless of race, creed, sex or sexual preference. The prostitute's reverence for the dead was misplaced; it didn't help you catch killers, it left the killers free to keep on murdering. Santillo and Weston saved their reverence for the living, not the dead, so they kept on doing the disagreeable task until they were finished.

Then they took turns standing where the redhead had stood, and sighting along their upraised arms to estimate the line of fire from the windows across the street. They figured that the most likely rooms were on the third and fourth floors, in the middle of the building. The windows in question occupied the west side of a hotel managed by an oily guy with slick black hair and manicured fingernails, who just *knew* Santillo and Weston must be mistaken. There could not have been a sniper in *his* building.

"This is a residential hotel," he explained, prissily stroking his mustache with a clear-polished thumbnail. "Our clients are not wealthy, but they are honest citizens."

"I'm sure they are. It's not too likely that one of your residents took pot shots from his own room," Santillo patiently explained. "It was probably an outsider. He could have got into one of the unoccupied rooms overlooking Eighth Avenue."

"But all of the rooms on the west side are occupied."

To prove this the manager took out a floor plan and accounted for the occupant of each room.

"How about this room?" Weston pointed to a small room on the fourth floor which the manager had skipped.

"Impossible," the manager assured them. "It's just an old employee locker room that we converted to a linen room. It's kept locked at all times."

The two detectives were on their way to the fourth floor before the manager had finished talking. They went up ill-lit stairs that stank of old urine and new disinfectant, and along the thread-bare carpet of the hall to the unnumbered door of the linen room. The door didn't look jimmied, but the lock was old and weak, and wouldn't have kept out a determined three-year-old. Chances were good that if this were the sniper's nest, the sniper would be long gone by now; but if a cop wants to live long enough to collect his pension, he doesn't take unnecessary chances, however slight they might be. So, guns drawn, the two detectives flattened themselves on either side of the door. Santillo silently turned the knob, then gave it a sharp shove and both men charged into the room, bent low to the floor, fanning out left and right to divide an enemy's fire.

But their enemy had already departed, leaving behind only the heavy smell of cordite in the muggy air of the little room. As in the past attacks, the sniper had taken the trouble to remove the shell casings. The two men looked over the room's wall shelves of linen and towels, but there was nothing out of place, nothing left behind.

Weston went to the window and took a look at the street below, where the crowds were being parted to let the first of the ambulances through. Its sirens whooped like an Apache once in warning.

Weston's eyes roamed over the bystanders. He started with the ones nearest the cordon, then moved out to the peripheral bystanders, and finally looked over those people as much as a block away who had spotted the commotion and had begun to be drawn toward it like iron filings to a magnet. He didn't know precisely what he was looking for; he was going on the feel of the situation. All his intuition told him that the sniper was the kind of man who might get kicks from watching the aftermath of his violent work, might be down there now watching the havoc. Men like the sniper enjoyed the commotion they stirred up, loved the feeling of power it gave them; they liked to walk among the innocent bystanders carrying their secret guilt like a hard-won prize. Weston was sure that this killer was like the pyromaniac who waits in the crowd to watch the flames he has brought into being, a worshipper at the altar of a self-made god.

Weston's eyes snagged on the scattered pedestrians half a block up Eighth Avenue, well beyond the spectators gathered at the sawhorse barricades.

"Vince," he called his partner to the window and Santillo took a look at the people down there.

At the scene of a crisis like this, most people tend to gravitate together to ask each other what's going on. The rest of the people either walked toward the scene because they're interested or away because they're not. Nobody—nobody with a clear conscience, anyway—would stand alone in the unlighted area between storefronts and just watch, the way a man was doing now. The red eye of a cigarette glowed from the mask of darkness his face wore. There was a dark blue beret on his head, and a leather satchel on the sidewalk between his spread legs. A satchel big enough, Santillo thought, to contain a dismantled rifle.

"I'll go down and get a closer look," Santillo said. "You keep an eye out in case he moves before I get down there."

Santillo took the service stairs three at a time, went through a fire door into the side alley, and walked quickly out to Eighth Avenue, whereupon he slowed to a normal pace. He walked out onto the street as casually as any man going for an evening stroll. The man in the beret was still there and flipped his cigarette in a long arc for the street where it landed in a splash of sparks.

There was nothing in Santillo's appearance to tip off the guy that he was a cop—in the alley he had removed the police badge, and was better dressed than cops usually were. But the guy in the shadows didn't judge a man by his clothes; he must have smelled cop, because as soon as Santillo started walking his way, the guy bent down, picked up his satchel, and started walking away up Eighth Avenue.

Santillo keeping apace on the other side of the street, picked up his speed a bit, and the man with the satchel did, too, as though he had eyes in the back of his head.

A crowded Eighth Avenue is not the ideal place to collar a suspect: there are too many passersby who could get hurt, and some—in this neighborhood—who might even intervene on behalf of the crook. But the man in the beret was too cagey to let Santillo get close enough for a collar: he waited until the traffic on the Avenue had reached a peak, then broke into a run up Eighth. Santillo would have been run down if he'd tried to cross the Avenue then, so he had to waste a few precious seconds waiting for a break in the traffic before he could give chase. This gave the beret time to turn the corner onto Forty-seventh Street and head west.

It was almost eight o'clock, the opening hour of Broadway's theatres and the pavement of Forty-seventh Street was a churning sea of theatergoers on their way from restaurants to plays and musicals. The beret disappeared in the midst of a huge crowd milling around outside the open doors of a theatre. Most of the crowd seemed to be waiting for someone to arrive; others were just talking, comparing notes on the dinner they'd just eaten, or just standing around looking elegant in their silver-trimmed tuxes and their ankle-length gowns with deep-cut jewel-studded bodices. It was a fashion designer's idea of the "in" crowd and it was a pickpocket's dream come true. Santillo raked the crowd with his eyes and spotted a couple of small-time dips plying their trade, but saw nobody carrying a satchel, nobody wearing a blue beret.

Santillo barged into the perfumed crowd. Up ahead he caught sight of a blue beret moving away on the sea of heads, and Santillo plowed after it, not leaving any newly-made friends in his wake. He was gaining on the beret when, as he got precisely in front of the theatre entrance, the crowd surged as one massive entity to meet a movie star's limousine that pulled to the curb, and Santillo was jammed to a standstill by the tightly-packed people. This was the event they'd been waiting for, and they all congealed around the limo to get a glimpse of the star as she got out. The sniper had got by the crush of people and Santillo could see the blue beret floating farther away down the street. But there was nothing he could do about it; he was pinned, and in seconds even the street was packed with people, bringing automobile traffic to a sudden and unexpected standstill.

There wasn't a free inch of sidewalk now. Collective gasps and murmurs were being released as the crowd got its first glimpse of the tall woman who stepped out of the limo into the flash of photographers' bulbs. And that beret floated farther away.

This was no time for politeness. Santillo wedged himself between a couple of women and started moving toward the street. In a few seconds he arrived at the side of the limousine gleaming darkly in the night's neon. There was no way around it, so Santillo climbed onto the hood, walked up the windshield to the roof and right down to the trunk. Shrieks started going up all around him, but Santillo didn't take his eyes off the beret. Jumping over people's ducked heads he landed on the next car back, another limo, scaled its windshield to the roof and right down to its trunk. He had to use another limo as a stepping stone before he got clear of the packed crowd of people, then jumped to the sidewalk. He was met by one of the limo chauffeurs, who grabbed him by the arm and angrily spun him around.

"You some kind of a wierdo, running on top of

cars like that!" the big man snarled at Santillo. "Don't you know who owns that car?"

"I'm a cop. I'm chasing a man. Now let go of my—"

"That doesn't give you the right to—"

The rest of the chauffeur's sentence gushed out in one painful exhalation as Santillo punched him in the stomach. Santillo jerked free of the guy's hand, turned and started running after the beret. The beret was a long ways off and had begun to run in earnest now, making no pretense of being just another man in a hurry. He was desperate to get away, barging through crowds and knocking people flat. But the satchel was slowing him down, and Santillo was gaining, now only half a block behind. The beret crossed Ninth Avenue and then Tenth on the dead run, Santillo right behind. It was less populous here, but there were still a fair number of people on foot, mostly pimps and their whores strutting their stuff. And they all decided to head for another part of town when they saw Santillo come barreling down the sidewalk.

The beret rounded a corner into an alley. Santillo got to the mouth of the alley a few seconds later, flattened himself on the sidewalk and looked cautiously into the alley. The pitted and crumbling cobblestone floor of the alley was littered with old papers and other trash that had missed the half dozen dented trash cans that stood against the left wall. On the right wall a single dim bulb in a wire mesh cage glowed above the padlocked back door of a restaurant. Santillo couldn't see anyone in the alley, and the only exit was at the back, where a board fence closed off the alley from the site of a building construction. There were some slats missing and Santillo could see through the gap to the dark pit that opened up on the other side of the fence, like a wound in the earth.

Santillo got to his feet. He unholstered his Smith & Wesson .38 snubnose and made sure that the safety was off. He was sweating from the strenuous run, and twice had to dry his wet palm before he got a grip on the gun; then, hunched down close to one wall, he entered the alley and made his way to the gap in the fence. He leaned against the fence a moment looking along the dark inside walls, and listening for sounds of movement, but all he could hear was the din of nighttime traffic on Tenth Avenue.

The fence encircled a deep hole with steeply sloping muddy sides. It dived perhaps fifty feet straight down into the dark, moist earth. At the bottom, part of the foundation had been poured, and gleaming in the faint light, the sharp points of reinforcing rods could be seen reaching up from the foundation into the night. There were concrete forms and bundles of reinforcing rods lying around the site, but no sign of any living thing.

Instinct. That was what saved Santillo's life. There was no reason to suppose that the beret was behind him, but Santillo suddenly knew that he was back there, felt it with absolute certainty. If the beret were back there, it was a safe bet that his intentions would not be very beneficial to Santillo's health.

Santillo dropped to his knees in the dirt and rolled sideways along the inside wall of the fence.

At least that's what he tried to do; but as he was moving, there were already two bricks flying through the air at him. He dropped below one that would have cracked his skull open, but the second one hit him in the shoulder and slammed him forward enough so that instead of jumping sideways along the fence as he'd wanted, he was falling into the pit. His hands grabbed wildly for a hold in the slimy mud, but he couldn't find one, and he slipped down so that he was clinging to the steep wall like a fly. He held on a moment, unable to move without sliding farther down. He heard the beret's footsteps as the man walked calmly out of the alley. Then Santillo slid down a bit more. Then slid again. The farther down the sloping wall he got, the steeper the slope became. Another couple of feet and the wall would be vertical, and then gravity would clutch him in a strong hand and pull him right down onto those reinforcing rods which reached up like spiny fingers. They would not leave a nice corpse for Santillo's mourners to view.

He slipped another inch, then two. The fall seemed inevitable. Santillo held his breath, hanging on for dear life, but the slow slide continued. His sweating palms hastened the slide. Santillo's back already began prickling in anticipation of the reinforcing rods....

As soon as Weston saw Santillo appear on the street below, he left the hotel's linen room and headed for Eighth Avenue; but by the time he had returned to the street, there was no sign of his partner. He walked up Eighth, but couldn't pick Santillo's face out of the milling crowds. On the corner of Forty-sixth he button-holed a pimp in a wide-brim leather hat with a peacock plume in the band. The guy had a woman on each arm.

"Have you seen a guy wearing a blue beret, carrying an Adidas satchel?" Weston asked.

The pimp had already pegged Weston as a cop, and answered with a curt shake of his head, as though humoring a retarded child.

"Not me, man, I ain't seen nothing since—"

"Yeah, I saw him," said the woman on his left arm, a ginger-haired black with the spaced-out eyes of a junkie on a high. She didn't notice the pimp's shut-your-mouth-whore look, and she was too young and new to the street to realize you never gave anything to anybody—least of all information to a cop.

"Where did you see him?"

She jerked a thumb toward the corner of Forty-seventh and Eighth Avenue.

When Weston got to Forty-seventh, he heard the shouts and exclamations of the people in front of the theatre, caught sight of Santillo running across the tops of the limos. Weston tried to catch up to his partner, but plowing through the crowd was not an easy task, and by the time Weston had emerged on the other side of the crowd he had completely lost sight of Santillo. Further down the street there was no one running or even walking fast. Weston wandered down that way, crossed Ninth Avenue, then Tenth. Still no Santillo. Weston asked a young couple passing by if they'd seen two men running by but they were in love and hadn't seen anything but each other since the evening had begun.

In the middle of the block Weston stopped in the mouth of an alley. He looked down it to see a dark gap opening in a wood-slat fence at the far end.

Would beret try to hide in there, Weston wondered. Weston might have gone down there to take a look, but at that moment he caught sight of the beret further down the street, walking swiftly toward the side door of an eight-story parking garage. The man with the beret still had the satchel in one hand, but didn't have Santillo on his tail, and in spite of the heat of the evening this sent a chill up Weston's spine. Police detective partnerships are like marriages in many ways: they are based on mutual dependence, affection, trust, and respect, and out of those feelings a closeness akin to familial love develops. The best partnerships are made in heaven *and* hell and are just as satisfying as a good marriage —only they are twice as rare.

So when a cop's partner is hurt or in danger, it's a little like a threat to one's own wife. The thought that the beret had hurt or killed Santillo put vengeance in Weston's veins, and he took off after the guy on the dead run. He got to the door of the parking garage before it was pulled shut by its pneumatic hinge. He stepped into the relative cool of a concrete stairwell, pulled the door closed on the street noise and stilled his rasping breath so that he could pick up the footsteps of the beret.

Scritch, scratch; scritch, scratch.

He was on his way up, and when Weston looked up at the stairwell he saw the man's shadow swinging across the walls as he ascended. Weston went up the stairs soundlessly, keeping away from the banister so that the beret would not see him if he happened to look down.

Scritch, scratch; scritch, scratch.

Weston had made it to the second parking level by the time the noise of footsteps stopped, and chanced a glance upward: the guy's shadow was disappearing on the seventh level, one below the roof. Weston took the next five stories on the run, pulled open the door, and went through at an angle, hunched down, his .38 Smith and Wesson in his hand.

The beret was nowhere to be seen. No *scritch, scratch*, no car engine running, no shadows moving between the parked cars. Quiet as a graveyard.

Weston started walking the ribbed runway between rows of parked cars. Beyond the cars, his own shadow accompanied him on the bare concrete wall. Traffic sounds filtered in from outside. But there was no sign of anyone else in the garage.

Halfway down the lane an automobile engine coughed into life, but the sound echoed off the walls so that Weston couldn't tell which car had been started until the big new Chevrolet a few cars away leaped out at him like a rodeo bronc leaving the stall. Weston didn't have time to do anything but fling himself to one side, and only just managed to do that before the Chev was thrusting its front end across the spot where he had been standing.

He landed hard on the concrete, rolled left as the Chev's front end swung into the lane and started bearing down on him. Weston kept on rolling. The pursuing front wheel of the Chev was gaining on him, but he managed to roll under the grill of a parked Lincoln—rapping his head hard on the filthy underside—just as the Chev smashed into the Lincoln's grill. The Chev backed up, then surged into the Lincoln again, like a persistent dog lunging at a rabbit hole. Then, as if giving up, the beret kicked the Chev into reverse, backed up, and burned rubber getting away down the lane.

Other cops might have left it at that, content to let the guy get away, feeling lucky that they'd escaped with no more damage than a bruised forehead and an oil-stained suit jacket. But other cops weren't Weston: all he could think of was that his partner might be lying bleeding to death somewhere, and that the bastard in the Chev was responsible. A man in Weston's line of work held two things sacrosanct: his family and his partner's welfare, and not necessarily in that order. So Weston scrambled out from the Lincoln, reached his .38 where it had fallen and—lying flat on his stomach—he steadied his hand on the floor. He let off two shots in rapid succession, the second of which hit the right rear tire blowing it out with a report like a rifle shot. The Chev limped to a quick halt, idled a moment, as if in indecision. Then the reverse lights went on and the Chev started limping back straight at Weston, its two red lights glowing like the eyes of a madman. Weston took out the other back tire with a single shot, then rolled—to the right this time—and got to safety under the front end of a Mercury as the Chev's rear end swerved after him and slammed into the big car. It rammed the Mercury a couple more times, as though in anger, then it left, its wheel rims chewing into the concrete and spitting out sparks and chips of cement as it went. Weston crawled out from under the car and started running after the Chev.

The Chev swung onto the spiralling down ramp, disappearing around a corner pillar. Weston hit the ramp at full tilt, and was almost down to the next level when suddenly the ramp was filled by the dark form of the Chev coming back up the ramp in reverse. Weston was moving too fast to change direction, but even if he had not been, there was no place to go to avoid the car, except straight up one of the building's big concrete support pillars, so Weston acted on impulse and ran a step or two directly at the car, then jumped like a broad jumper. The Chev charged under his leaping body, and Weston landed on the car's trunk, his momentum carrying him halfway onto the roof. Weston grabbed the roof coping and held on as the Chev's rear bumper punched a wall. He was still holding on when the Chev started limping back down the ramp. The Chev gathered speed for a moment and Weston braced himself for the fall that he knew was coming. When it came, it was sudden and merciless. The beret—at top speed—twitched the steering wheel sharply to the left, then back again, and Weston was thrown from the roof like water from a shaking dog. He hit the pavement and was thrown into a pillar so hard it knocked the breath out of him, and for a moment all he could do was sit there trying to get his abdomen to draw some much-needed air into his lungs. Then he saw the Chev had swung full circle and—headlights glaring—was bearing down on him. Weston decided that breathing could wait. He pivoted around the pillar and a split-second later the side of the Chev sideswiped the pillar, dragging its metal side against concrete with an ear-tearing screech. The Chev came to a rocking halt, then charged back at him and Weston had to dive under the nearest car, a low-slung Toyota that barely gave him clearance.

The Chev rammed the side of the Toyota, reversed, rammed it again, and the second time the Toyota scooted sideways under the impact, forcing Weston to scoot along the floor in order to stay under the car.

The beret didn't give up at that. He put the Chev in low and floored the accelerator and the big Chev started moving the little Toyota sideways right off of Weston. Weston didn't have any options: he grabbed the suspension coils with his hands and hooked a leg on the rear axle and was dragged along with the car, as the Chev pushed it across the parking garage. Weston hung on for all he was worth, hoping the Toyota was not so small that it would just flip over onto its side like a sick dog and leave Weston exposed to the lunging Chev. It didn't. It left a stinking trail of hot rubber all across the garage, but it stayed upright.

The Toyota came to a jarring stop at the wall. The Chev reversed, then charged the Toyota, then repeated that pattern again and again, a metal monster gone mad, as though it hoped to smash the Toyota flat against the wall so that it could get at Weston, who was still wedged under the small car, gradually getting covered with dirt and dried mud and corrosion that rained down on him from the undercarriage each time the Toyota shuddered under impact.

After a couple minutes of this, the Chev backed up and came to a stop a few yards away. There it waited for a while, lights full bright on the mangled Toyota, engine chugging hesitatingly, like a mutant beast trying to catch its breath before resuming its attack. Seconds drifted slowly by, and Weston began to feel claustrophobic under the mangled metal that once had been the Toyota: the frame had buckled in places, giving Weston no more than an inch clearance in some spots, but he couldn't afford to move, not with the Chev's headlights spotlighting him as soon as he stepped into the open.

Weston wiped the soot and flakes of dirt from his eyes, then squirmed around onto his back and pulled his .38 out of his waistband where he had hastily stuck it before the attack had begun. He didn't have a good line on the car from where he lay, so he crawled forward a bit, then leveled his gun at the left headlamp. He took out both lights in two quick shots, and waited a moment for his eyes to grow accustomed to the dark. When his night vision had returned, he could see that the driver door of the Chev was standing open.

Beret was out on the street by now, having left the empty car's engine running to menace Weston, like a Doberman guard dog. Weston felt like a damn fool, as though he'd just been intimidated by a toy poodle or a Chihuahua. He hauled himself out from under the Toyota, which took a couple of exhausting minutes because of the buckled frame, and went over to the empty Chev.

The sniper had departed in such a hurry that he had left his beret behind. It must have fallen to the car's floor when he was ramming the Toyota and he had not taken the time to look for it before leaving. Weston picked up the hat. It wasn't much of a reward for a night's work, but it was more than anybody had got from the sniper's first three attacks. There was no telling, maybe the lab boys would come up with something.

Weston took a look at the Chev's registration. As he was leaning across the front seat of the idling car he heard the scrape of a footstep behind him. He spun around, bringing his .38 up to meet a short paunchy businessman holding a briefcase with one hand and his young secretary with the other.

He looked wild-eyed at Weston and, shrill as a hysterical woman he screamed: "What have you done to my car!"

Sliding down, beginning to feel the implacable pull of gravity, the internal organs involuntarily clenched in anticipation of those reinforcing rods below—like being in quicksand, where every movement toward safety only draws you deeper into the inevitable suffocation. Like life itself, a slow backward slide to death, inevitable, irreversible.

Santillo knew he had about thirty more seconds before he had slid down the slick slope to the point where he was totally at the mercy of gravity. Until now, he had just been holding on, hoping that Weston would catch up with him, or that a passerby would stumble across him. But hoping wasn't good enough; he had to take control of his own fate, act before it was too late.

He lifted his right leg and kicked the point of his shoe straight at the muddy wall. The movement caused him to slip another couple of inches, but his foot went deep into the earth, digging its own foothold, and he stopped the slide. Quickly he did the same with his left foot, a little higher up than the other, and now he was almost rock-steady. Carefully he withdrew his right foot, then kicked it into the slope a little higher up. Then the left foot again, and he had risen inches up the slope. He kept working at that arduous climbing. It took him a full twenty minutes, and twice his footholds gave out and he slid back a few feet; but eventually he made it to the rim of the pit, and dragged himself to the safety of the alley. He lay there in the suffocating heat of the night air, staring up at a sky where the stars were out of sight above the city's neon glare. He was exhausted, arms and legs like leaden stumps, his body covered from head to toe with caked-on mud that had soaked through his clothes to the skin. He would have liked nothing better than to curl up in a corner and sleep the night away; but he remembered the sniper, then thought of Weston, and he slowly climbed to his feet and left the alley.

Pedestrians were still thronging the pavement, but none of them gave so much as a glance to the man who looked like he'd just spent the night being churned around in a cement mixer filled with mud. Being New Yorkers, however, they had a highly developed sense for avoiding trouble, and even if they didn't look at him, they certainly gave him a wide berth.

Santillo made his way through the crowds to the flashing lights of a prowl car parked in front of the parking garage down the street. He caught sight of Weston—disheveled and covered with dirt—leaning against a black-and-white.

Smiling wryly, the two cops looked at each other in silence a while. Only the most astute observer could have detected the outward signs of the relief the two men felt upon seeing each other alive and reasonably healthy.

"I'm chasing a goddamn killer," Weston commented wryly, "and you wander off somewhere just when I need you. What the hell have you been up to? You look like you have been trying out a grave."

"That's pretty close to the truth," Santillo said. "Did you get the bastard?"

Weston told him what had happened, then looked his partner up and down, taking in the caked-on gray clay that was beginning to dry in places, and obscured half his partner's face.

"I think I've changed my mind," Weston said thoughtfully.

"About what?"

"About your clothes," he answered. "I think gray does suit you after all. If only it covered more of your face..."

3

"This makes C.A.T. look like a very select branch of the police department, a very élite corps," Lt. Hunt grumbled sarcastically at Santillo and Weston. He held up the morning edition of the *New York Times*, so that both his detectives could get a good look at the picture on the front page. It showed an evening-gowned movie star looking in utter horror at Santillo who was running across the top of her limousine. The photo caught him in mid-step, and made it look as if he were doing a tap dance. The accompanying article contained some coy comments about Santillo's "ill-advised attempt to break into show business," and then went on to describe in great detail how the episode had upset the star so much that she had fainted and been unable to attend her famous husband's premier performance on Broadway. Precisely the kind of publicity the police department—and Lt. Hunt in particular—loathed. Lieutenant Hunt went on:

"You do a tap dance on four limos, scare a movie star half to death, and beat up her chauffeur."

"I identified myself as a police officer and the guy still tried to stop me from—"

"I don't want explanations or excuses," Lt. Hunt snapped. "I want to know how I'm going to justify this kind of performance to the commissioner." His steely glance shifted to Weston. "And you—five minutes in a car park and you total two brand new cars. What is it with you two, and why cars last night? What's it going to be tonight? You going to pick on motorcycles, or maybe stereos? Whatever it is, make it something inexpensive, huh?" He blew out a disgusted sigh and shook his head wearily.

"You're right, lieutenant," Weston agreed. "When the sniper came at me in that Chevy, I should have had the sense to hide behind something cheap. Maybe there was a cardboard box lying around somewhere that I missed."

"You guys never learn," the lieutenant growled. "We're running a police department here, not your private destruction derby. C.A.T. was set up to help protect the citizens of this city, not give them another thing they need protection from. God knows there are enough of those around already. I want you guys to be more discreet, a little more—*sensitive* in your dealings with the public. Walking on cars, for Christ's sake—and not just any old car, but a celebrity's limo, surrounded by photographers!"

"We're supposed to just let the guy get away?" Santillo protested. "A few chips out of a celeb's limo's paint job is worth more than the five women lying dead two blocks away? Since when?"

"He got away, didn't he? And what have you guys got to show for it—not even a vague description. You found out the sniper's a man. That's a real valuable discovery! Oh, yes, you captured his beret single-handedly. Thanks a lot. The beret is liable to give us another big zero, and you can bet your ass that his satchel will be in today's garbage, so we can forget about that." He sighed again. "All I'm asking for is more—sensitivity."

Lt. Hunt got to his feet. "Right now I want you guys to meet your new partner, Matt Christian. He's in the gym downstairs. Come on."

They followed Lt. Hunt to the exercise room in the basement of headquarters. It was a large room with barbells and dumbbells and exercycles and other fitness equipment arranged along the walls. In the center of the room, wrestling mats were arrayed to create a small arena. When the three cops arrived, the arena was occupied by two men in judo whites.

One was a powerfully-built black man not much smaller than a house. The other was Matt, a fresh-faced youth with the muscled upper arms and chest of a practising weightlifter. He was not tall, and next to the towering black man he looked downright frail; but he was incredibly quick and easily able to dominate the larger man. Santillo and Weston looked on in astonishment as Christian's agile movements and his fast, darting fists soon had the bigger man baffled and frustrated in defeat. It was an impressive display of fighting talent. At the end of the one-sided bout, the two fighters bowed politely to one another. Then Matt Christian walked over to one corner of the room where a four-by-four piece of lumber was supported between two concrete blocks. Christian squared himself in front of the blocks then —as though to demonstrate what he could have done to his opponent if he had wanted—he brought his hand down like an axe and broke the four-by-four in two.

Lt. Hunt called Matt Christian over, and introduced him to Santillo and Weston. Christian was one of those guys who liked to squeeze hands to pulp when he shook and Lt. Hunt smiled serenely at Santillo and Weston's grimaces of pain.

"Matt's joining us from Homicide North, where he was handling the model murders," Lt. Hunt informed the two detectives. "He'll be with us until we get our two cases off the books. And please keep in mind—all three of you—I want these investigations conducted with a bit of delicacy."

Lt. Hunt returned to his office. When Christian was dressed in street clothes Santillo and Weston took him upstairs to their own office, a windowless room that was just big enough to contain their two desks and one filing cabinet. The room was hot enough to fire clay pottery, and Santillo and Weston were rolling in sweat. But Matt Christian didn't show a drop of perspiration, and didn't bother to follow the other cops' lead by taking off his coat.

"I like the heat," he told them, and as though to prove how comfortable he was, he offered up his first smile of the day: a lop-sided bearing of teeth that was more like a sneer.

Christian filled them in on the progress he'd made with the investigation of the murdered models. There were a few details that were new to Santillo and Weston:

"Both of the first two models killed had received threatening messages before the crimes," Christian said. "The first one got a letter saying she was going to get hurt. The second one got a phone call. The guy described how he was going to cut her up. And sure enough that's what he did to her. I ran a check this morning on the latest model, Melissa Martin. If she did get a threatening call or letter, she didn't bother filing a report with the police."

"Even if she didn't it still looks like the work of the same killers," Santillo said. "Same m.o.: renting the hotel room sight unseen, the mutilations with the knife."

"I'm not so sure," Christian said. "There was no indication of sexual intercourse in the first two killings."

"True, but—" Santillo was interrupted by a call from the lab. He scribbled some notes, then hung up and conveyed the information to Weston and Christian: "Prelim on Melissa Martin. Nothing interesting except for the fact that she had sex with at least three different men in the hotel room."

"Three!" exclaimed Matt Christian.

"That's right. Analysis of seminal fluid showed three different blood types."

"So the m.o. is different," Matt Christian declared. "She wasn't killed by the same guy as the other two."

"Not necessarily," Santillo said. "It could be that—"

"What do you mean, 'not necessarily'?" Matt Christian scoffed. "There were at least three guys with Melissa Martin. You can bet those guys weren't with the other models, or they would have banged them."

"Agreed. *They* weren't. But the *killer* was."

"Huh?"

"The killer has been getting bolder with each

killing. The first two times he just killed the women. Maybe with the third one he decided to watch some guys bang her before he killed her."

"It's possible," Weston agreed. "The men who did bang her probably don't even know about the killing. They'll read about it this morning, and be too scared to tell anybody what happened."

"I suppose it could have happened that way," Matt Christian admitted grudgingly.

They threw other possibilities around, but Santillo's guess seemed the most likely, and until something better came along it would be the working premise.

Santillo and Weston spent the next half hour filling Christian in on the snipings, and kicking around ideas about the man responsible for them, but came up with a big zero on everything: motive, psychological profile, ideas about his next attack.

"All we've got to go on is that beret," Weston concluded, "and the lab won't be finished with it until this afternoon at the earliest."

"We're wasting our time here," Santillo said. "Let's hit the streets. Matt, why don't you and I work together on the model killings while Wes does some digging on the sniper action?"

"I'll work on the sniper with Weston," Matt Christian announced.

"Well—okay. But I thought that since you already know the model killings from working on them at Homicide North—"

"I'll do my own thinking, thanks," Christian said tightly. "I'm working with Weston."

"Don't I have a say in this?" Weston asked lightly,

attempting to lessen the tension. But Matt Christian was as humorless as he was stubborn.

"Sure," Christian proclaimed. "If you want to, you can work the models with Santillo, and I'll handle the sniper on my own."

"Where did you get your genius for diplomacy?" Santillo inquired mildly.

"I don't like to be pushed around," Matt Christian told him. "It riles me, and watch out when you do that," he added with a defiant look.

"What do you do then, break a brick with your black belt?" Santillo took up the challenge.

"Yeah. The brick between your ears."

"Easy does it." Weston stepped between the two men and did his best to smile in spite of his urge to bury a fist in Matt Christian's sweetly bland face. He wondered what Lt. Hunt would say if their new partner was carried out of here on a stretcher less than an hour after the first meeting. *Besides,* he thought, *I'll have to work with the belligerent jerk, and I might as well make the best of it.*

He guided Matt Christian to his feet and urged him out of the room. As he closed the door, he gave Santillo a smile and the thumbs up sign, but the grim look stayed on Santillo's face. "I suppose you think the martial arts are a joke, too," Matt Christian asked Weston on the way to the elevators. "You and Santillo are living in the dark ages, you're being out-moded. You have to have the same special training as the terrorists and other scum who are turning this world into a pile of shit."

"Is that what makes you so much fun to be around, all that special training?"

"You laugh, okay, but you have to have training. You miss a trick and you're dead. Hell, you saw what I did to that poor sap in the karate room. A criminal could do the same thing to you. What happens if a guy comes at you, a guy who knows karate or judo? What do you do?" Matt Christian laughed at the thought. "You're all but defenseless."

"I guess so," Weston agreed without much interest.

They got into the elevator and started the ride down.

"Don't patronize me," Matt Christian said tautly. "I'm serious. I could kill you with my bare hands. Hell, with *one* bare hand. What would you do if I came at you right now?"

"Well," Weston said thoughtfully, "I guess I'd just plant a .38 slug right between your eyes."

Matt Christian didn't ask any more questions of his new partner.

Santillo's first stop was Melissa Martin's agent, a gaunt woman in her seventies who told him that Melissa did almost all of her modeling at the Jenkins Studio. Santillo found the Jenkins studio on upper Madison Avenue, in a high-rise whose tinted windows gave off a murky reflection of the cloudless sky. It was another stifflingly hot day. The sun was sitting overhead pouring almost unbearable quantities of heat and light onto Manhattan, bleaching the sky almost white, its every reflecting surface hurting the eyes.

The studio occupied most of the twelfth floor. A plantinum-haired receptionist presided over a roomful of beautiful women whose eager faces all turned to smile at Santillo when he entered the room, as though they expected somebody special. Then they returned to their magazines and paperbacks when they saw he was just another man. Santillo waited a few minutes while the receptionist talked with somebody on the phone, then was led down a corridor to the office of the owner, Miles Jenkins, a deeply-tanned man with diamond rings on each pinkie, who was filling the room with smoke from a big black Havana cigar.

"I was appalled to hear about poor Melissa," Jenkins said piously. "But I really don't think I know anything more about the dire circumstances than anyone else. I wish I did. I'm sorry I won't be able to help you much. We used Melissa a couple of times this summer, layouts for *Fashion Today*, *Modern Fashion*, *Avanti!*, that sort of thing. She was a great worker, got along well with the photographers, and the other models, too, which is pretty damn rare in this business. Believe me, there are usually lots of petty rivalries and jealousies, but she stayed away from all that."

"Do you know if Miss Martin had received any threatening letters or phone calls recently?"

"I have no idea." That was Jenkins's answer to every question that Santillo posed. After a while Jenkins sneaked a quick glance at his watch and said, "I'm late for a meeting right now. Would it be all right if we continued this a bit later?" Without waiting for an answer Jenkins got to his feet, all smiles and whirling cigar smoke, and ushered Santillo to the door. "Sorry to cut things short like this."

"Maybe I could talk to some of the models who knew Melissa—"

"Not right now, I'm afraid," said Jenkins as he

deftly tucked two Havanas into Santillo's coat pocket. "The models are all working in the studio at the moment, but my secretary will give you any names and home phone numbers you want."

The next thing Santillo knew he was standing alone outside the door with only the smell of Jenkins's Havanas to keep him company. Annoyed, Santillo took the two cigars the guy had given him, broke them open, and crumbled the tobacco on the carpet. Then, instead of walking out to the reception room, Santillo headed the other direction, passed through two doors, and found himself in the studio, a huge open space that had been broken up into smaller areas by portable, hinged partitions that didn't reach the ceiling. There was a maze of these doorless enclosures encircling the main photography area where Klieg lights stood in a semicircle around a backdrop of sky blue paper.

Six models in colorful raincoats and open umbrellas were moving around against the blue backdrop. A photographer trailed around after them, occasionally crying, "Hold it!" and snapping two or three photographs while the models held the pose. Then they moved around again until, by chance or design, they hit another configuration the photographer liked, and he took some more shots. The methodically shifting models and photographer were the calm eye of a hurricane of activity, as all around them, in the darkness outside the lights, dozens of people were busy preparing lights and cameras and scenery for the next setup, or frenetically wheeling in and out of the maze with clothes on racks, or delivering photographic supplies.

Santillo watched the photographer work for a

while, then he wandered off. He passed a room where four models were getting out of drably-colored baggy slacks and wrap-around blouses that apparently were some designer's idea of high fashion, but made these beautiful women look like off-duty circus clowns.

Santillo excused himself for intruding on their privacy, and was about to move on when one of the women came over to him and asked for a light. This normally did not cause Santillo's knees to turn to water, but this time it did, for two reasons: one, this tall blonde was one of the most beautiful women he had ever laid eyes on; and two, at the moment she was wearing nothing but a pair of lace panties. He snapped flame under her cigarette. He smiled uncomfortably a moment, trying to coolly keep his eyes above her shoulders, but then he thought, what the hell, and looked down at her fine body. His look seemed to amuse but not embarrass her. Nor were any of the other models embarrassed to have a man standing around lighting cigarettes while they were undressing.

"Christ, what a day," the blonde breathed out on a lungful of smoke. "And it's not half over."

"This a typical day?" Santillo's voice sounded a little funny to him, and added to her amusement.

"No, it's not. Normally strangers don't wander in and light my cigarettes for me. Who are you anyway?"

"Vince Santillo, N.Y.P.D. I'm investigating yesterday's murder of Melissa Martin. I'm looking for someone who knew her pretty well."

"You found your gal then: I knew her as well as anybody. We roomed together for a couple of months when we were just starting out in this business." She extended a pale firm hand for Santillo to take and introduced herself as Dawn Palmer. He liked the way her breasts moved when he shook her hand.

"You look a little bit surprised, Detective Santillo."

"I am a bit. I thought fashion models were, uh, skinnier."

She laughed. "You mean the skin-and-bones Twiggy look. No, that's been out for a while. Boobs are in this season. Thank God."

"I'll go along with that."

Santillo followed her across to a clothes rack where she selected a dress—a jet black arrangement of cords and beads and baubles that somehow contrived to make her look more undressed with the dress on than without it. Santillo zipped her up and she sat down in front of a light-ringed mirror. While Dawn put on some jewelry, the make-up woman came over and went about arranging Dawn's hair and touching up her cheeks and lips with dashes of color.

Santillo asked Dawn if Melissa Martin knew any of the other models who had been killed.

"No. She was due to pose with one of them, but got sick and couldn't make it. That was a few months ago."

"Did Melissa have any boy friends?"

"None who really scared her, if that's what you mean. Just the usual assortment of pests and perverts. The same as us all."

"She ever complain to you of threatening letters or telephone calls?"

"Not that I can recall—" She broke off and her face went still with remembering. "Well, yes," she added after a minute. "A couple of weeks ago she came in to a photography session all upset. She'd received something in the mail, she said. I was busy at the time and forgot to ask her later what it was. Is it important?"

"It could be."

"Maybe she told someone about it. I'll ask around."

A thin girl poked her acned face into the room and told Dawn that she was to go on in two minutes.

"That doesn't give you much time to ask me to dinner tonight, Vince," Dawn said to Santillo.

"It doesn't give you much time to accept either."

"But somehow I think you'll both manage," commented the make-up woman.

Weston and Matt Christian split up outside police headquarters, Christian going to interview the owner of the Caddy limo that had been seen leaving the latest sniping, Weston returning to the hotel to see if he could learn anything new.

The hotel linen room looked different in daylight, the sunlight revealing the dust on the stacks of linen and motes floating in the warm air. But that was all there was here: nothing had been left by the sniper.

"I really think you're mistaken about him using this room at all," insisted the hotel manager, who was trailing around after Weston like a puppy.

Weston stepped into the hall and then noticed a drop of fluid gleaming darkly on the floor in front of the door across the hall. He touched the fluid and it rubbed slick between his fingers: gun oil.

"What's this room?" Weston asked.

"Just a closet."

"Open it up."

It was a walk-in closet with detergents and cleaning agents on the shelves. But in the corner beneath the ceiling bulb Weston noticed a small stool and on the floor beside it were cigarette butts and ashes. The butts were arranged in the shape of a cross and lay on a circular bed of their own gray ashes.

"He must have bided his time in here waiting for darkness to fall before he went across the hall," Weston told the manager.

"What kind of man would make a design like that with cigarette butts?"

"An obsessed man."

As Weston turned from that corner of the room, a flash of color on a shelf caught his eye. It was the corner of a magazine protruding from beneath a detergent box. Weston lifted it and found a glossy porno magazine called *Hot Fox*. Picking it up by the corners to preserve fingerprints, he laid it down on the chair seat. The manager came over and watched Weston flip through the pages. It was standard fair for that rather limited genre: young, rather unattractive men and women depicted in virtually every sexual position in the *Kama Sutra*, and then some; showing men entering every female orifice with all kinds of phallic substitutes—and, often enough, the real thing. The striking thing about the magazine was what the owner had done to it: over every female model in the book he had drawn the same pattern he'd left the ashes in—a cross on a circle—the cross hairs of a telescopic sight. The cross hairs appeared on women's heads and over their hearts, but mostly on their genitals. You didn't have to be Dr. Freud to figure that one out, thought Weston.

Weston slipped the magazine into a cellophane

bag to keep it for the fingerprint men, then made a note of the brand of cigarettes the sniper smoked: Winston. Not much help there. Weston put a police seal on the door and notified the lab that they had another room to look at. Then he left the hotel and headed down Eighth Avenue to Forty-second Street, where he began a search for an adult book store that sold *Hot Fox*.

At any time of the year Forty-second Street is a carnival sideshow of the city's weirdos; though during an August heat wave it is worse than usual. Today it was wall-to-wall hustlers: pimps and hookers, pushers and junkies and silver-tongued con-men walking the sidewalks. Twenty-four hours a day, seven days a week, they would be there, one eye peeled for cops, the other eye peeled for the main chance. To keep these characters from walking off with everything that wasn't nailed down—including other people—a dozen uniformed cops were stationed in pairs along the strip, but even so you can't take five steps without some sly-mouthed guy offering, "Coke and smoke, coke and smoke," out of the side of his mouth, like a ventriloquist sideshow barker. The street is lined with massage parlors, adult theatres and book stores, cheap eateries, and fourth-run movie theatres with kung fu triple bills, where traveling salesmen kill time between appointments.

When Weston turned the corner onto Forty-second Street, there was a fight under way: two prostitutes were pulling each others' hair and kicking each other with pointed-toe shoes. A crowd had gathered around and were cheering them on while the beat cops took their time ambling over to break things up.

Weston went into an adult bookstore near the

corner of Eighth Avenue, a tiny place run by a guy the size of an overweight *soma* wrestler. The owner was sitting next to the cash register sweating as if in a steambath. Weston flashed his shield.

"You sell this magazine?" he asked, holding up a copy of *Hot Fox*.

The fat guy's face closed like a fist when he saw Weston's badge. He looked at the magazine, then said, no, he'd never seen the magazine before, didn't know anybody else who might sell it or had ever heard of it. There were a million and one different magazines—he couldn't be expected to keep track of all of them. This magazine was a new one on him, sorry officer.

He shrugged by way of apology, then put his nose back into the magazine he was reading when Weston had come in, expecting Weston to take the hint and leave.

Weston didn't plan on leaving until he got the truth out of this guy. He put his copy of *Hot Fox* into his jacket pocket, and walked deeper into the store. Pulling out a notebook, he started scribbling notes.

"What're you doin'?" The fat man was on his heels, sweating more than before, if that were possible, as he watched Weston note that the fire door was blocked by a book rack, and that the decrepit fire extinguisher merely exhaled a couple of gaseous sighs and then stopped working altogether.

"I run a clean joint," the fat man protested.

"But not a very safe one."

Weston walked deeper into the store, past the floor-to-ceiling magazine racks, and came to a dark hallway in back which was lined by a dozen private movie-viewing booths. A man and a woman were just entering a booth. Their voices could be heard as they started dickering over the price of her services. A moment later the dickering stopped and Weston could hear the man's noises of pleasure as the woman started those services. As Weston started to go over to the booth door, the fat man pulled the copy of *Hot Fox* out of Weston's pocket, then forced his own flabby face into an expression of surprise.

"Oh, *Hot Fox*!" he said. "Yeah, yeah, I recognize it now. What was I thinking of before!" Weston knew what he was thinking of now: his operating license. "Yeah, there's a store near Broadway that carries this mag. Mac's it's called. Only guy on the strip with that label, I'm sure." He smiled broadly. "See, we can be pals, can't we?"

"We'd be better pals if you cleared the fire exit, and got an extinguisher that worked. Today."

Back on the street there was another fight in progress, this one between two blacks who disagreed over the price of a bag of H. One of them was a tall skinny kid who was carrying a ghetto-blaster that blared punk-rock music at full volume. He held the big radio at arm's length in his left hand while he danced around throwing right jabs at his opponent. Tempers were short all along the strip, and as Weston walked toward Broadway, he passed a prostitute as she kneed a john in the groin because the guy had the gall to wonder aloud whether her talents were worth the high asking price.

Mac's was a hole in the wall between a photograph studio and a café that belched out the thick foul smell of grease. The interior of Mac's was dark, the sunlight cut off by green plastic curtains that gave the place the underwater look of an aquarium. The darkness didn't stop the proprietor from wearing wrap-around sunglasses. He was a greasy-haired guy in a colorful short-sleeved shirt, and sergeant's stripes tatooed on his left arm.

"*Hot Fox?*" the guy said after Weston had identified himself. "I guess we sell it, yeah. So what? I don't remember who buys what in this joint."

"Did you sell this particular issue?" Weston asked, holding up the copy.

"I really couldn't say. Maybe I did, maybe I didn't." He leaned across the high counter and spilled mint-scented breath at Weston. "You got to remember, it's important for us to maintain the privacy of our clients. There's no law against buying these magazines. And I'm not breaking any laws by selling them. So why don't you take your questions and shove 'em?"

"I'm looking for a killer."

"Look all you want, just don't drag me into it."

"You're already in it, punk. For all I know the killer I'm looking for might have sergeant's stripes tatooed on his arm. He might use axle grease for shampoo and wear sunglasses in dark places. That description sound familiar?"

"I ain't no goddamn killer!"

"You sure aren't an honest citizen eager to help the police in their investigation. That makes you a suspect."

The guy gave it a moment's thought. "Lemme see that magazine," he said, and studied it for a minute before saying, "It wasn't sold here. We stamp all our magazines across the page ends and this one hasn't been touched. I don't see any store's mark, so maybe it was bought direct from the distributor."

"Who distributes *Hot Fox?*"

"Hot whores," the guy joked, then got serious: "Company named Fox-E, Enterprises. A local company. They're into mags and films, distribution and production. They got an office over on the Lower East Side." Weston got the address, then thanked the guy. "Oh, always happy to cooperate with the police," the proprietor commented sourly.

Santillo spent two hours and twenty minutes searching Melissa Martin's apartment before he found the threatening letter she had received. Starting in the bedroom, he cleaned out the desk, drawers and closet, then went into the living room where he looked in the wastebasket and between the pages of every book on the shelves. Finally, he searched the kitchen, and being a thorough cop, opened up the plastic garbage bag sitting near the back door, emptied it on some newspapers, and then waded his hands into the mess. He picked the letter out of coffee grinds and moldy orange peels. The envelope—a large manilla, bearing stamps cancelled in Manhattan—contained an 8 x 10 magazine photo of Melissa Martin modeling a fish-net dress that did very little to conceal her body. The sender had marked up the picture with a red pen, having drawn a dotted line running across her throat; red globs of blood dripped from the line. "I'll cut along the dotted line," was printed across the top.

And that was exactly what the guy had ended up doing.

On his way out of the apartment, Santillo bumped into an old codger with flaring side-whiskers and the stooped posture of the very aged.

"You are going to get the bastard that killed her?" the man demanded.

"We'll do our best," Santillo answered. "Did you know Melissa well?"

"Yes. A sweet girl. Busy as she was, she always had time to humor an old man with some cheerful talk. It's a real tragedy when death takes a person at that age, a real tragedy. And especially with her so close to the big break she'd been waiting for."

"What big break is that?"

"It was kind of a secret. She was being considered as the model for a big magazine spread of some designer's latest creations. She figured it would make her known, a real break, and then this had to happen."

Santillo questioned the man some more, but all he learned was that Melissa Martin had not informed her own agents about the assignment. There were two possibilities: the assignment was simply a figment of Melissa's imagination, something to impress the old fellow with, or that the assignment was connected with the murder. A way of luring Melissa to the hotel room where she had died, perhaps?

The more Santillo thought about this killer, the more disgusted he felt. He wanted to nail this guy in the worst way.

Matt Christian did not like the looks of the man who got into the elevator with him. The guy was an Arab; swarthy, pock-marked face, nose like a knife blade. Christian didn't have anything against Arabs, but this guy was different—there was something about him that didn't sit right with Christian, something about the deep-set black eyes that made Christian keep a sharp eye on the guy as the elevator started rising toward Abdul Abidi's penthouse suite.

The Arab got off two floors below the penthouse, and Christian went the rest of the way by himself. Two Arab men sitting on chairs outside the penthouse rose to meet Christian when he came over. They said he couldn't go in without first giving up his gun.

"I'm a cop," said Christian. "Where I go, my piece goes."

"That means you don't go in to see the hakim."

"This is the U.S. of A., buddy," Christian told them. "You want to make up your own rules, then stay in your own goddamn country."

One of them tried to answer this objection, but before he could get a word out, Christian moved, shoving an elbow into one guy's stomach while he snapped his foot into the other man's groin. Both of them were on the floor holding their mid-sections and moaning when Christian opened the door and walked into the penthouse suite. He was met by Farah, who was pointing a .45 automatic at Christian's head.

"N.Y.P.D.," Christian identified himself quickly. "I want to talk to Abdul Abidi."

"About what?"

"His limo was seen leaving the scene of the sniping last night."

"I can explain—"

"Let's have Abdul explain it himself."

Farah led Christian to the bedroom, where the

hakim was lying on the satin sheets of a large circular bed. Two women who had just climbed out of bed were getting dressed in the corner of the room. The smell of hashish was almost overpowering.

"Your limo didn't waste any time getting away from the scene of the sniping last night."

"Yes," admitted Abdul Abidi. "When the first shot was fired we thought it was intended for Farah."

"Why did you think that?"

"I have enemies in this country," Abdul Abidi told him. "I was deposed by a revolution and barely escaped with my life. The new regime in my country has got it into its head that I must be returned to my native country to face a tribunal. They have dispatched some men to the U.S. to try to take me back. By force. This team of kidnapers is led by a man named Yusef Ramad. I thought at first that it was Ramad who was shooting last night."

Christian remembered reading about the hakim's reign of tyranny: after twenty years of his bloody dictatorship, he had been deposed, escaping from Sabindi with virtually all of that little country's national treasury already tucked away in his own numbered Swiss bank accounts. The few national treasures that he had not already sold for cash on the European market, he managed to take when he fled the country. This included twelve gold statues studded with diamonds. Value: sixteen million dollars. Not surprising that the poverty-ridden natives of Sabindi wanted him brought back.

Christian asked: "What does this Ramad look like?"

Farah give him a description. It matched the one of the Arab who had come up in the elevator with Christian.

As Christian left the apartment, Farah admonished him: "Your tone with the hakim was impertinent."

"In this country he's not a hakim, he's not even a citizen, he's just a visitor. He wants to be a hakim again, tell him to return to his own country."

"You are being very impertinent, even to a visitor."

"Let's just say I'm not wild about visitors who bring their civil wars along with them."

Christian took the elevator down two floors, then walked down the hall in the direction Ramad had taken earlier. All the rooms along this hall were offices occupied by established firms. Ramad was long gone, having probably waited for a few seconds and caught the elevator on its way down.

Christian left the high-rise and returned to police headquarters at 1 Police Plaza. He stopped at the crime lab in the second basement. The report on the sniper's beret was finished and it yielded a couple of interesting facts: the sniper had brown hair and used a medicated dandruff shampoo.

"We got a partial thumbprint from the plastic band inside the beret," a lab technician told him. "Not enough points for a positive i.d., but the guy has a burn scar on his right thumb. That should help you guys some."

It would help *me* plenty, Christian corrected the lab technician in his own thoughts. It would not help Santillo and Weston because Christian had no intention of showing this report to Santillo and Weston. Christian was looking out for number one, and he could do that by keeping to himself any clues to the sniper's identity.

"Don't bother sending any other sniper reports to

the C.A.T. office," Christian told the lab technician. "I'll drop by every night to pick them up."

"Suit yourself," said the lab technician. "You're keen on this sniper case, aren't you?"

"Let's just say it would not hurt my career any to wrap up the case fast."

Ambitious son-of-a-bitch, thought the lab technician. This was one analysis he decided to keep to himself.

Weston arrived at Fox-E, Enterprises, during the filming of a romantic epic called *Long Dong Silver's Revenge*. When Weston walked into the studio, the film shooting was at a standstill: electricians, sound and lighting technicians, cameramen, director, and three or four actors and actresses were standing around waiting for the film's male star to get it up for Scene 7, Take 2. The leading lady was doing her best to get him prepped, but it seemed to be a losing cause, and after a while she freed her mouth from him and leaned back, fed up and annoyed.

"Dead meat," she said disgustedly. "I can't get a rise out of him."

"I'm not a machine," declared the leading man. "I've got to know my motivation for this scene."

"Here's your motivation." His co-star spread her legs and pointed to her crotch.

"I'm serious," he said. "I have to know what moves the character I'm playing."

"Ex-Lax," she retorted.

"It's easy to see why no director will let you play a scene when your mouth isn't full."

"Knock it off, you two," warned the director. Then

he signalled one of the other actresses, and she came over to go to work on the leading man.

Weston asked one of the idle electricians who was in charge of the studio and the guy pointed to a man in a black suit who was pacing up and down in agitation—a pudgy man who couldn't have topped five feet. He was talking to himself when Weston walked over to him.

"I'm paying fifteen men union wages to stand around doing nothing because that jerk can't get hard on cue. So what if he's hung like a horse? If he can't get it up when we need it, what's the point? Nobody's going to buy a five dollar ticket to watch it just hang there! Oh, this goddamn movie's going to ruin me! I'm going down the tube because of a goddamn limp dick!" He stopped his harrangue when he saw Weston. He said, "Cop, right? I can spot you guys a mile away, while I'm looking the other direction. Hey, Laura! Come here." The leading lady put on a robe and came over. "Honey, we got a cop here. Take a couple minutes and make him happy."

"Get bent," Laura told him. "I'm an actress, not a whore."

"You peddle your pussy on camera instead of on the streets. Big difference."

"There is a difference," she asserted. "Read my contract if you don't believe it." She turned around and huffed away.

"How this goddamn business has changed," the short man lamented to Weston. "Used to be, if you paid the salary, you had some say in what went on, but not now. Now they're *stars*! Bullshit. Hang on a sec, though, officer. I'll have one of the other gals—"

"I'm not interested," Weston told him. "If I want to get laid, I know where I can do it."

"So what do you want from me?"

"Information," said Weston. "You distribute a magazine called *Hot Fox*, don't you?"

"What of it?"

"Which store did this copy come from?"

"This legit? You're not here just to knock off a piece of tail?" For a moment he stared incredulously, as if Weston were a beast with two heads, then shrugged and turned his attention to the copy of *Hot Fox*. "We supply a dozen outlets in Manhattan," he said after a while, "but this magazine issue didn't come from any of them. They all put a special stamp on the mag somewhere and this one is unmarked. This one must have come straight from us. We sell some of our own mags and photos in a little shop we run upstairs. There's a gal in the place now, maybe she can help you."

As Weston was turning to leave the studio, a cheer rose from the stagehands around the set: the male star strutted onto the set ready for Scene 7, Take 2. *Long Dong Silver* was ready for his revenge.

A street door led up a flight of stairs to Fox-E's small magazine store with its walls covered with magazines in cellophane wrappers. The tall redhead behind the cash register had a knockout figure, the kind of body that forces a man to clear his throat before he'll trust it not to jump an octave when he speaks.

"May I help you?" she asked Weston.

Weston cleared his throat. He showed his shield and asked her about the copy of *Hot Fox*.

"It was sold here, all right," she agreed. "We

haven't sold many of that issue." She counted the copies on the shelf, and concluded that Weston's copy was the only one sold. "I don't remember the man who bought it very well," she added. "Dark brown hair, kind of youngish—twenty-five, say. Clean cut. I can't picture the face, but I remember feeling that the guy was strong, powerfully built."

"Would you recognize him if you saw him again?"

"I might."

He got her name—Jessica Newman—and home phone number, in case he had to get hold of her again. As Weston was walking out, a man brushed by him and swaggered over to Jessica.

"You stood me up last night, honey," he accused.

"You again? I told you to get lost. Just because you buy a magazine, doesn't mean I have to go out with you."

He grabbed her by the arm and pulled her into his arms, allowing his hand to trail across her breasts.

Weston went over and grabbed the guy's hand and bent it backward at the wrist and the guy yelped like a kicked dog, and let go of Jessica Newman, but Weston kept on bending the wrist until the guy had to go down on his knees to keep his arm from breaking.

"I think you owe the lady an apology," Weston said.

"I don't owe her—ow! Okay, okay!"

When he had apologized, Weston let him up. The guy scampered to the door. He turned around to say something tough, but decided against it when he saw Weston's face.

"Thanks," Jessica said when the guy was gone. "It's not often you come across a guy who'll give a woman a hand when she needs it, instead of when she doesn't."

"I'll give you a hand any time."

"You got my phone number, didn't you?"

"Yeah..."

"Well, dial it sometime. Soon."

Dawn Palmer writhed on her back on the mat floor of the studio, while a photographer moved around her, his camera clicking furiously to catch her mobile face in one pose after another, blond hair swinging in a gentle spray across her sea-green eyes. She writhed and he followed, and Santillo and everyone else in the studio stood stock still watching, rapt, hypnotized by the erotic beauty of her movements. It took over ten minutes to get enough photographs to satisfy the man with the camera and when the session finally ended, both he and Dawn Palmer were covered in sweat. They lay as limp as rag dolls on the mats for a minute or two before Dawn got up and walked over to where Santillo was standing.

"Great session, Dawn!" the photographer called to her, and then got up and hustled the film into the dark room.

"I need a long shower and a short drink," Dawn said to Santillo, "and then we can get something to eat."

"I know a great place in Little Italy—"

"No Italian food," Dawn demurred. "Pasta doesn't like me. It goes straight to my hips and makes me look like I'm wearing a bustle on each hip. And in this racket hips are poison."

Twenty minutes later she came out of the dressing

room and started to head for Santillo when a tall blond guy with a camera draped around his neck stopped her.

"Dawn, I watched your session, you were terrific as usual," he said.

"Thanks, Mitch."

"You have a way of moving your hips ... sensual stuff ..." Mitch Roundtree's blue eyes held hers for a moment.

She waited for him to go on talking, but he didn't seem to have anything more to say, just watched her, and she began to feel uneasy. In spite of his good looks there was something about Roundtree that repelled her. And she did not trust him. More than one of the models he had dated a while back had been forced to cancel photography sessions because of black eyes and bruises. He was the type who blamed his personal problems and failures on women, and that was the kind of guy Dawn Palmer could do without.

She started to walk past him, but he maneuvered to cut her off.

"Isn't it time we got together for dinner, Dawn?"

"I don't think so, Mitch."

He launched into a steady stream of requests for a date, but Dawn kept shaking her head, no. After a while she lost her patience, shook herself free of him.

"One of your admirers?" Santillo asked when she'd joined him.

"You could call him that, I guess. He's a staff photographer here, a very good one, as a matter of fact. He's also something of a creep, he gives me the willies. He's been nagging for weeks for a date and it's starting to bug me. The jerk just wants to get into my pants." She gave Santillo a swift look. "I'll bet you'd like to, too, wouldn't you?"

"Uh, well..."

"Go on, admit it, you'd like to get into my pants."

"Well, uh..."

"Well, you can forget it, not tonight," she said, and then her stern look turned into the kind of smile that melts a man's spine as she leaned close to Santillo and said, "Tonight, you see, I'm not wearing any..."

Mitch Roundtree watched Dawn Palmer leave the studio on the arm of the cop, watched the way she smiled warmly, the way she leaned toward him, and he felt anger rush through him like cold fire. She had turned him down flat so that she could throw herself at a cop! Roundtree's palms itched; he wanted to soothe that itch by wrapping his hands around Dawn Palmer's throat... he could imagine his hands on her neck, and his fingers clenched in frustrated anger around the lens cap he was holding, and the hard plastic cap bent in his fierce, strong grip.

The bitch, he thought, *treating me the same way Melissa did*. The same way they all did... he put an "x" by her name in the notebook he carried in his mind. He thought about how her eyes would widen in fear when he would draw out his knife, and the thought made him go rigid in anticipation.

"You all right, Mitch?" This came from one of the models who had just come out of the changing room.

"Fine," Mitch Roundtree answered, forcing a smile through his clenched teeth. When the model left he walked into the changing room and found Jane Turner putting on her street shoes. She frowned on seeing him, as though sensing trouble.

He said, "Jane, there's something I'd like to talk to you about—"

"If it's about the date we had, Mitch, forget it. That could happen to any guy—"

"It's not about that," he said quickly. "It's about a job. I've been asked to do the photo layout for Signon Lancia's fall line. He wants me to use one model, and naturally I thought of you..."

"Lancia originals!"

"Not so loud," he admonished. "You know Lancia and his rep. He's an eccentric designer and doesn't want any word to leak out, least of all about using only one model for the entire line. He's got a whole new concept ready for the fall, and he doesn't want anyone to breathe a word of what's going on. You know how in this business there are types who would steal any idea..."

"Sure, mum's the word."

He watched light come into her eyes as he talked, and he knew that he had her, and couldn't keep from smiling as he pictured how she'd look when he took out the knife....

4

At six P.M. Weston met his wife Ellen on the steps of the Metropolitan Museum of Art. He would rather have been meeting her between the sheets of their double bed, but she was on a campaign to make herself, and especially Weston, cultured; so tonight they were scheduled to attend a concert of Baroque music which was to be played on some of the museum's 17th century instruments.

"This is a real event," said Ellen, who just that afternoon had boned up on Baroque music and was eager to share her learning with Weston. "We were very lucky to get tickets for this concert."

Weston felt about as lucky as a blind man at a silent movie, but he smiled dutifully and marched up the museum's broad steps with her. Halfway up there was a stir on the street as a silver Cadillac limo pulled to the curb, its occupants ushered out of the car and up the steps by a small squad of the museum's administrative personnel. The V.I.P. was none other than the hakim, Abdul Abidi. A tall, thin man whose goatee was salted with gray, the hakim was dressed in the turban and long-flowing robes of an Arab potentate.

A couple of the museum security staff held all visitors to one side while the museum administrators hustled the hakim up the steps and into the building ahead of everybody else. When Weston and Ellen finally were allowed through the main doors, they found the museum curator and half a dozen people from the mayor's office in the lobby bowing and profusely thanking the hakim for visiting the museum.

"Why the song and dance for him?" Weston wondered out loud. "Just because he graces the museum with his royal presence?"

"No," Ellen answered with a smile, "but because he's gracing the museum with his royal presents. As in gifts. He's donating some of his country's national treasures to the museum. I think it's his way of trying to buy citizenship here. And it might work. No one seems to care that the gifts are not his to give away. They belong to his homeland. Or did until he stole them."

Curious, Ellen wandered over to get a better look at the hakim, while Weston paid for the tickets. As he was turning from the desk with the tickets, he noticed a trio of swarthy men along the far wall who were watching the hakim with interest, their avid dark eyes full of black anger. They were trouble, Weston knew. He looked around for Ellen, who was standing in the small crowd gathered around the hakim.

"Ellen," Weston called casually, and waved for his wife to come over, but she was too interested in the goings-on to heed. Weston went over to Ellen, keeping the trio of Arabs in the corner of his eye.

The trio split up, fanning out around the entrance lobby, their eyes staying on the hakim. Weston reached his wife, grabbed her by the arm and gently but firmly guided her toward the doors.

"Wes, where are we going?" Her amused eyes went grave when she saw Weston's grim countenance, and she knew there would be trouble. As he pushed her out through the doors she pleaded, "Wes, come outside with me, if there's going to be trouble here. Please."

"Get somebody to keep people from coming in through these doors," he told her, "then find a phone and dial 911."

When she was safely outside, he turned back to the lobby, but the trio of men had disappeared. The hakim was being ushered down a long wide corridor leading to the museum's offices. Armless torsos chiseled by ancient sculptors stood under each of the enormous paintings lining the corridor. Weston started down the corridor, but he had taken only three strides when a harsh voice erupted the austere silence, stopping the hakim's group cold in their tracks:

"Don't take another step!"

The voice belonged to a squat man with close-cut black hair, and the hard, flat black eyes Weston had seen countless times before on hired killers, eyes that are depthless, opening forever into a soul black as sin. He was built like a block of granite, square and solid and hard as any one of the ancient statues that stood around watching the scene unfold.

"Ramad!" gasped the hakim, and the squat man smiled acknowledgment.

"It is I," Ramad said. "I promised to take you back

to Sabindi and I shall. You will stand trial for your traitorous acts to Islam and you will repay what you have stolen from our land." Calmly, without a word of warning the silenced automatic in Ramad's hand spat flame and one of the hakim's bodyguards dropped lifeless to the floor like a sack of flour. "If anyone else reaches for a gun he will meet the same fate. Now, Abdul, if you want to spare us unnecessary bloodshed, you will step over here and come away peacefully."

But sparing blood—other than his own—was the farthest thing from hakim Abdul Abidi's mind. He pushed one of the museum directors into the line of fire, and made a run for the nearest door, diving through it, his robes billowing around him like turbulent white clouds. None of Ramad's trio of accomplices fired at the man, they wanted him alive. They began to follow him into the room but they were suddenly frozen by the clamorous ringing of a fire alarm. To cover his escape with a confusion of people, the hakim had pulled the alarm, and now all hell broke loose. Doors flew open all around and the museum staff and visitors, thinking the building was on fire, came pouring out into the hall, heading for the exits. They flooded past Ramad and his accomplices, creating bedlam. Ramad and his men gave up on the hakim and used the cover of the crowds to leave the corridor. Weston and two of the hakim's bodyguards followed the four men into the main lobby, where crowds were streaming toward the main doors.

One of the bodyguards got excited, and pulled out his gun and took aim at one of Ramad's men. Weston pushed the guy's gun hand up and bullet exploded into the vaulted stone ceiling just as a couple of old ladies teetered around a corner and into the line of fire.

"Keep that gun holstered until these people get out of here," Weston commanded.

Ramad and the other three knew there would be cops waiting outside, so instead of heading out the main doors they went deeper into the building. Weston and the bodyguards elbowed through the crowds in pursuit.

Weston might have had scruples about firing into a crowd of innocent people, but Ramad's men did not. Two of them turned in unison and started pumping slugs from twin .45s and suddenly the air was thundering. A man dropped across Weston's path clutching his side in pain, and a woman was spun around by a slug, a red stain spreading like dye on her back. Screams went up, and now men and women alike were running with the selfish determination of outright panic, unheeding of anyone's welfare but their own, trampling people in their frantic effort to escape.

Ramad and his men turned a corner and took a flight of steps up to the next floor. Weston got to the stairs in time to see them disappear through a door on the right. He went up the stone steps two at a time. One of the bodyguards had been caught in the confusion downstairs, but the other was right on Weston's heels.

When Weston was halfway up the stairs, two of Ramad's men appeared at the top of the stairs and leveled their .45s at Weston and the bodyguard, who were completely exposed. Weston threw himself flat on the stairs as a slug ricocheted off the step he'd been standing on and tunnelled into the wall, kicking up a shower of stone dust. The bodyguard wasn't as fast to react. He was just going into a crouch when a slug caught him in the chest and lifted him into the air like a giant hand. He landed on his back with a crunching sound, and toppled slowly down the stairs.

Weston got off a quick shot that hit one of the men. The stunned Arab grunted and clutched the hole in his stomach, then pitched forward down the stairs. His partner went down on one knee and started pumping slugs at Weston, the first hammering the wall by his arm, the second creasing the air overhead. Weston was too exposed to last long where he was, and there was no cover on the stairs. In fact the only thing in the tapestry-hung stairwell besides Weston himself was the dead Arab rolling head over heels downward. But in a situation like this one, a man uses whatever is at hand; so Weston braced himself on a step and timed his roll perfectly: swinging feet out and up, he kicked off from the wall and rolled across the wide stairway just as the dead Arab's body was rolling past, and Weston met it with enough momentum to stop its descent. He twisted around and crouched behind the dead man as though behind a bunker.

The Arab at the top of the stairs let one more shot fly—a wild one that ripped into a tapestry high overhead—then ducked back into the doorway on the right. It looked as though he were running to catch up with his two friends: that was what he wanted Weston to think anyway, because a few seconds after he had disappeared he jumped back out, his .45 blazing. He had expected to see Weston, unshielded, rushing up the stairs, a sitting duck for a .45, but instead what he saw was Weston still bunkered behind the dead man. Weston's .38 Police Special was trained on exactly the spot where he'd appeared. The Arab fired twice in panic before Weston's first shot slammed him between the eyes and his forehead collapsed into his skull.

Seconds later Weston was stepping over the dead man and into a long exhibition gallery filled with medieval religious paintings on the walls and religious statues standing on pedestals in wall-niches. Not so much as a chair for a man to hide behind. At the other end of the gallery Weston paused at the door and listened. The alarm had just stopped its wailing. The visitors had cleared off this floor, and there was a lot of noise coming from downstairs, but there was no sound on this floor to tell him which direction Ramad and the fourth Arab had gone. Then a thin metallic noise sounded above the muffled din from downstairs. The tinkling of glass.

Weston moved in the direction of the sound, through a room with walls covered with tapestries, into a room crammed with all manner and styles of furniture. The furniture was arranged in groups around the exhibition room: sitting room, bedroom, dining room, each encircled by a red velvet rope to keep visitors from standing too close. As Weston moved through the room he saw a dark form behind a huge wing-back chair—a woman, huddled on the floor, trembling and sobbing in pain. It was easy to see what was hurting her: she must have stood between Ramad and something he had wanted, for he had smashed her across the lower jaw with the butt end of his pistol, opening up a gash that ran from ear to chin. She was holding a handful of her teeth and trying to stem the flow of blood with a handkerchief. She motioned to the door at the end of the room.

"In there," she said. "Never mind me. Get those bastards."

Weston led her back to the safety of the next room, then he went back to the door she had indicated.

The room was in complete darkness, and it took Weston's eyes a moment to adjust to the point where he could tell that the room was full of medieval arms and armor. Chain mail vests and iron visors gleamed on the dark walls beside bulky breast plates and embossed shields. Suits of armor stood upright in the corners. Hung on the walls and standing in glass cases were medieval weapons of every sort: bows and arrows, crossbows, bludgeons, and hammers, mallets and axes, swords and spears. Everything the well-dressed warrior could ask for.

Weston moved along the left-hand wall until he came to a long corridor. On one side, a row of phantoms in suits of armor stood like a ghost army awaiting their leader. Across from them a row of windows, between which were more weapons in glass-topped table cases.

One of the windows had been broken and a length of rope anchored to the sill and dropped to the ground outside. Weston went to the window and looked out. In the distance he could see the squat Ramad running for the darkness-shrouded foliage of Central Park. Weston was about to climb out the window and lower himself by the rope when he saw a reflection move briefly in a piece of broken glass still clinging to the window frame: a man's head, floating as though disembodied in the darkness behind Weston. Ramad had left the fourth Arab behind to make sure that he was not followed.

Weston dived to one side. A shot echoed behind him and a slug kicked into the wall where Weston had been standing. The slug ricocheted freakishly, rattling off a piece of armor and then knocking over a quiver of arrows that rained down on Weston, jabbing his arm painfully. Reaching for his .38, Weston found his hip holster empty. He'd lost the gun when he jumped away from the window. There was no hope of finding the gun in the dark room, and Weston didn't have time anyway: even as he was spinning out from under the arrows, Ramad's man was sending a couple of slugs at him.

Weston rolled across the floor, came to his knees behind one of the armored knights. He shoved the knight at the Arab, and as the creaking pile of armor toppled onto the guy, Weston launched himself in a low dive, hitting the killer a split-second after the armor did. The three of them went down in a thunderous metallic crash. The Arab swung the gun down to Weston's head, but Weston hit the gun with a piece of armor that he had picked up and the gun spun off into the darkness beyond the windows. The Arab kneed Weston in the stomach, then, locked arm-in-arm, they rolled into another phantom knight in armor. The knight dropped its metal knees into Weston's back, and then the rest of it came crashing down, a bruising, unwieldly mass of wrought metal.

By the time Weston had freed himself from the heap of metal, the killer had retreated along the wall and grabbed one of the long-handled battle axes hanging on the wall. He swung it overhead like a lumberjack and brought it sharply down. Weston dived to the wall and the axe-blade clanged off the concrete floor beneath the carpeting. The killer swung again, and this time Weston had no place to move to—all he could do was yank up the breastplate of the fallen knight and the blade rang off the metal like a dinner gong. When the Arab wound up for another swing, Weston heaved the breastplate at the guy's head, and that gave Weston time to scramble across to the far wall where he could put some distance between himself and that axe. Weston got to his feet. The killer moved in on Weston, holding the big axe like a baseball bat. Weston pulled a shield down from the wall and slipped his arm into the leather strap. The Arab wound up and swung the axe again. Weston got the shield up in time to ward off the blow, but the axe hit with such force it dented the metal and nearly knocked Weston off his feet. The Arab swung quickly, before Weston could fully regain his balance, this time trying to swing the blade under the shield for a shot at Weston's legs. Again Weston blocked the blow with the shield, but this time the metal buckled and the axe-blade nearly sliced through. If Weston was lucky, the shield might ward off another blow, but it certainly couldn't take two more. But Weston didn't need to worry because the Arab was finished swinging the axe and found a surer weapon.

As he advanced toward Weston. The Arab's foot brushed an object on the floor and he looked down to see Weston's own gun lying there. The Arab didn't have to think twice about which weapon he preferred: he threw the axe down and went for the gun.

There was no place to retreat, Weston was stuck in the middle of the long corridor and a good fifteen feet separated him from the Arab, too much ground to cover before the Arab had the gun in his hand. Weston acted without thinking. As the battle axe was falling to the floor, Weston took a couple of steps forward and dropped the shield through a glass case that stood nearby. He reached in through the jagged shards and pulled out a short-handled battle axe. As the Arab was bringing the gun up off the floor and working his finger in through the trigger guard, Weston threw the battle axe.

The weapon might have been old, but it was still beautifully balanced for throwing and deadly as any modern weapon. The axe-blade caught the guy in the forehead and the razor-edged metal cleaved his head, burying itself right where his right eye used to be. For one grotesque moment the guy defied death and reared to his feet, the axe-hilt angling out of his skull, and he wavered in the moonlight streaming in the windows. Then he gave in to the relentless pull of death and toppled over backward.

Weston, exhausted and aching and bruised, sat down on the floor and rested a minute before he picked up his gun and made his way back downstairs.

Dawn Palmer chose the restaurant, a small place with hand-hewn wooden tables and chairs, a beamed ceiling and lights so fashionably dim, the waiter must have needed a seeing eye dog to get around. The place was full of models and aspiring actresses and actors squinting into the darkness to try to spot an agent or producer who could give their careers a boost.

Dawn ordered quiche and a spinach salad, and Santillo tried to order a steak, but the waiter just gave him a sneering smile and informed him this was a vegetarian restaurant.

"Okay, bring me a vegetarian," Santillo said. "Medium rare."

Dawn laughed, a low musical sound that pleased Santillo like good Italian wine. As he watched her pretty face he noticed for the first time with a stab of surprise that Dawn's nose was slightly crooked; it took a little wobble to the right on the way from brow to tip: the imperfection that capped perfection. It was a modest flaw, and by the time a man got around to noticing it, he'd already taken in more than enough other details to compensate.

All through dinner they talked and drank wine; as the wine level of the bottle decreased so did the talk and they ended up just looking at each other in the dim light, feeling the warm tinglings of sexual attraction. Out on the street they cut through Central Park on their way to a subway station. On the gravel path Dawn stopped and looked up at the moon. Then she looked at Santillo.

"You know what we're going to do now?" she asked, a pleasant wine slur in her voice. "We're going back to my place, have a nightcap—"

"Or two."

"—or three, and then we'll probably make love. How banal."

"Sounds okay to me."

"How trite, routine," she went on. She hooked her

arm through his. "I want tonight to be something different. Besides, my air-conditioner is broken down."

"And I don't have one..." He took her in his arms and kissed her, felt the darting warmth of her tongue against his. She pulled away and then took him by the hand and led him off the path, outside the cone of a streetlamp's light. She nestled in the darkness under a maple tree.

Santillo brushed her lips with his own, sent a trail of kisses down her neck into the sweet hollow of her shoulder and he could feel her breath quicken as she pressed against him. He cupped her breasts through the thin material of her dress and he felt her nipples harden to pebbles of flesh in his palms. Her ragged breath was hot in his ear, her tongue a warm and insistent thing.

He cupped her buttocks and pressed her to him, and she caught her breath when she felt the hardness of his groin.

"I want you right now, Vince. Now," she insisted, pulling him further back into the dark shadow of the tree.

She leaned up against the trunk, hooked her fingers in his belt and pulled him closer to her. She unzipped his pants and her fingers were a feather touch on his skin. He hoisted her skirt and found that she had told the truth about not wearing panties, the thick triangle of blond hair gleamed in the faint light like the beckoning nest of some exotic bird.

She pulled at his pants and then gasped when his cock leapt free of the restraints and pressed up against her. Holding her at the back of the thighs he lifted her off the ground until he could feel the wet warmth of her sex, then he lowered her slowly and heard her groan as he entered her. He lowered her further and her moan deepened as he penetrated further into her warm wetness. She clung frantically to him, her breath coming in hard uneven gasps as he moved her up and down, quickly at first, and then slowly, as he could feel the erotic heat building in his loins, then slower still, extending the sensual pleasure. Minutes trickled slowly by as the couple were both lost in the heat of their own embrace. Then Santillo felt the tension growing in Dawn, felt it drawing her tight, tight, tighter, until the intensity of the feeling could not be contained any longer and it burst free, and her body convulsed in orgasm, and convulsed and shuddered again, and again, as pleasure swept over her in wave after wave and finally left her limp and weak, a meek smile on her sweating face as she clung to Santillo.

As he paused for a moment, still buried deep within her, she started clenching her vaginal muscles and they undulated against his hard shaft and the fire in his loins grew warmer. He stirred within her, then the lure of pleasure urged his hips into motion again, and a few seconds later he came too, an overwhelming, draining orgasm that seemed to pull from the spine and wrenched a moan of pleasure from him in spite of his efforts to remain silent. Another spasm, and another and then the two of them were leaning, spent, against the tree gasping and sweating in the warm evening air.

After a time, Dawn got her breath back, and she grinned and said, "Wow."

Santillo couldn't argue with that assessment.

● ● ●

Dawn Palmer lived in the upper 80s on the East Side. Her apartment was an old stone and brick building dwarfed by towering high-rises on each side. Santillo and Dawn Palmer took the elevator to the seventh floor. They had taken a few steps down the hall when Dawn stopped and pointed down the hall to where light spilled out through an open door onto the blue-patterned carpet.

"My apartment door is open!" She started for the door, but Santillo held her back. He told her to stay put as he drew his .38 and went down the hall alone. He waited outside the open door a moment, hearing nothing but the hum of a refrigerator; then he spun through the doorway into the small studio apartment. There was no one in the room.

The room looked perfectly normal, nothing out of place; in fact, no indication at first glance that the place had been broken into. Dawn followed Santillo into the room a moment later, and let her glance move across the convertible couch, the stereo and records on the wall shelves, the framed photos of herself with her parents on the coffee table, and the little kitchen nook where washed dishes were drying in a plastic rack.

"Nothing seems to be missing," she said. "But I'm sure someone's been in here. I remember locking the door and I know I didn't leave the lights on."

Santillo tucked his Smith & Wesson into its shoulder holster, then turned to face Dawn.

"Maybe the janitor—" Santillo began, and then stopped as he looked over Dawn's shoulder and saw what neither of them had seen before: a photograph of Dawn had been pinned to the inside panel of the door. It was a blow-up of an advertising shot;

it showed her in a skimpy dark bikini holding up a tube of suntan lotion.

Dawn spun around before Santillo could stop her and saw the photograph and gasped. The blood drained from her face when she saw the photograph had been disfigured: the beautiful body was marked with lines of red ink that sectioned her into pieces like a side of beef. Red globs dripped from the inky incisions. Across one side of the picture—in the same regimented printing that had appeared on Melissa's defaced photograph—were the words:

"A piece of meat, ready for the knife."

"This is a pretty sick joke," Dawn said in a choked voice.

Santillo didn't want to tell her it was no joke, not just yet. He grasped her shoulders and turned her away from the photograph, and gave her a comforting hug before he led her over to the couch to sit down.

"Who do you know with a sick sense of humor?" He tried to make it sound light, but she recognized his underlying tension. She started to answer, but she checked herself when she heard a faint sound from outside; it could have been a woman's scream.

Santillo went out into the hall, listened: it was a scream, all right, but it was not coming from any of the rooms on this floor, it filtered down from above.

"The roof," said Dawn.

"Call the cops," Santillo told her. "And lock yourself in your apartment. Don't open up for anybody without asking for i.d."

"You're not going up there by yourself?" she protested, but he gently pushed her back into her apartment, waited until she had locked the door, then he went to the stairway door at the end of the hall, and climbed two flights of iron-slat steps to the roof door. The screams were more distinct now and he could hear other voices, men laughing.

He opened the door a crack and looked out across the dark roof. Near the parapet two punks were holding a woman spread eagle on the asphalt for a third guy who was lying on top of her. Santillo stepped through the door with his .38 drawn, and walked quietly across the heat-softened asphalt to within a few feet of the three rapists.

"Freeze, you bastards!" he said, and all three punks froze, turning astonished faces up at him. "One of you bastards so much as *thinks* about making a sudden move, and you'll be swimming in your own blood."

"Easy, man," one of them said softly. "Easy, We're just having ourselves a little fun."

"Next time have it with somebody who wants your kind of fun. Now get on your feet. Hands against the parapet, legs spread, you know the position."

The woman—a girl, really, hardly out of her teens —rolled sobbing and shivering out from under her attacker, and crawled a few feet away. She was too upset to notice the fourth man on the roof until the guy had got right next to Santillo and by then it was too late. The guy swung a bicycle chain like a whip at Santillo's gun hand and the hard-surfaced, articulated chain snapped around the big compact Smith & Wesson, biting painfully into Santillo's fingers. The chain pulled back, yanking the gun out of his hand and flung it skittering across the roof.

The four would-be rapists quickly formed a circle around Santillo to cut off any retreat, and then with a quick theatrical movement they pulled out knives and flicked the spring blades open to gleam in the light from surrounding buildings.

"Now, we're gonna have a different kind of fun," one of them said, and the four slowly began to close in on Santillo.

They were hopped to the gills, Santillo could see it in their dilated pupils, in the dreamy drone of their voices, the dreamy smiles that hung on their pale faces. That made them dangerous, but it also made them vulnerable because it distorted their perceptions, made them feel an inordinate and unrealistic power. And when that happens, when you think you have complete and irreversible power over a man, then you will let down your guard, and that is the time he will strike.

Santillo arranged his face in a mask of fear, and put a whine in his voice as he pleaded: "Wait, please. Don't—don't hurt me, please. Don't. I didn't mean what I said, I was just, you know, I was just..." He went on babbling for mercy like that, making his voice shake, and he could see them believing the act. He detected in their advancing bodies the slight relaxing of vigilance that comes when an attacker thinks his victim presents no threat. They were grinning broadly at his fear, almost laughing at the way their own great power had reduced a cop to this.

Santillo backed away from one pair of attackers. His line of fear-stricken babble made them think that he was unaware that he was backing straight into one of the other punks, but he knew it all right, was judging his distance from the punk by the faint shadows on the roof. When he was three feet away he pivoted quickly and swung a right cross at the guy, slamming his right fist into the guy's stomach, and blocking the guy's knife hand with his left. As the astonished guy doubled over, Santillo brought his knee up sharply into the guy's face, and felt the guy's nose collapse against his knee cap.

Santillo pushed the guy into one of the other punks, then bent over and picked up the dropped knife. While Santillo was bent over, one guy lunged, but Santillo had expected this and he side-stepped and lashed the guy's arm with the point of the knife. A red line opened up and poured blood across the guy's forearm. These punks hadn't expected a cop to be much of a knife fighter, but Santillo had grown up in the poor section of Little Italy—a neighborhood where you either learned to handle yourself or you figured out a way to live the rest of your life in your room. Although Santillo had done his share of street fighting with a blade as a kid, he'd never really liked knives, and it had been years since he'd handled one like this. But as soon as he felt the smooth handle in his palm, he felt all of the old instincts come back.

The other two punks felt them too, and they warily moved around him now. They stationed themselves on opposite sides of Santillo, and their movements were more guarded. The quick blood and violence had brought them a bit down from their dope highs. They were still grinning their spaced-out grins and dreaming of blood, but they were dangerous now. They worked as a team, and they were good.

They moved in on Santillo from opposite directions, always keeping the detective between themselves, so that he could not watch both of them at the same time. They'd done this sort of thing before, obviously, and it must have worked well, because they were playing it to perfection tonight. As they moved closer to Santillo they started to give him feints. First one punk, then the other, would give a little half-lunge, pulling back quickly, and watch the direction Santillo moved.

Santillo tried to keep moving, but there was no way to avoid being stuck between the two of them. Then—as sirens started up in the distance—the two guys went still, and Santillo knew the attack was coming. The guy on the left was the first to move, a quick lunge with the knife outthrust like a sword. But that was just part of their act—when Santillo turned to face this attack, the other punk made the killing move, charging hard and fast.

Santillo spun full circle, stepped inside the lunging man's swinging knife. He grabbed the guy's arm, snapped it back at the elbow, and it broke like a dry bread stick.

The second guy lunged. Santillo jumped back, and the punk's wildly swinging knife went hilt deep in his friend's chest. The guy stared in amazement at the wash of blood. His eyes lost their focus, and the dreamy grin came back to his mouth. He continued to stare at the blood as though hypnotized. Then he let loose a wild laugh, pulled the knife out and plunged it back into the stricken man. And then did it again, either not knowing or not caring or being too hopped up to care what he was doing, he plunged it again. All his drug-hazed brain knew was that it was fun to watch the red roll out of this man's stomach.

Santillo stepped behind the guy and slammed a fist into his temple, and the guy went down like a pole-axed steer. Santillo took away the knives and cuffed him and his two wounded pals to the man who'd just been stabbed to death. Then he put his coat over the young girl's naked shoulders and took her down to Dawn's apartment. Dawn calmed the girl down while he put in a call to headquarters and asked them to send for an ambulance and the morgue wagon.

"You and Weston are really cooking tonight, aren't you?" exclaimed the police dispatcher. "I just sent a squad car out to the Met. Seems Weston did a number on a couple of Arab-types. All in a knight's work, huh? Get it. A knight's work—"

"Is Wes okay?"

"Yeah, a couple of bruises is all."

Santillo went back up to the roof and found one of his prisoners crying like a baby. It seemed he was scared to death of being handcuffed to a dead man. He didn't have any qualms about making him dead in the first place, he just didn't want to be forced to look at it afterward.

"His blood's getting all over me!" the guy screamed hysterically.

"That tends to happen when you stab a man," Santillo told him.

It was after midnight before the cops had taken away the would-be rapists, delivered the intended victim to her parents in the building, and left Santillo alone with Dawn in her apartment. Santillo unpinned the threatening photograph from the door, placed it in a sandwich bag to preserve fingerprints.

"It's serious, isn't it? It's no joke." Dawn Palmer wanted to know.

"What is?"

"That photo, the threat."

"Serious enough that I think you shouldn't spend the night here."

"I don't have anywhere to go . . ."

"I've got a double bed."

She packed an overnight case, and they cabbed over to Santillo's apartment in Little Italy, a small cheerless place that suited him just fine. It wasn't until after they were settled in his place that she broke down, tears coming in big gasping sobs that racked her whole body. She knew what her carved up body in the photograph meant.

"It's the guy who killed Melissa and the others, isn't it?"

"I'm afraid so."

He spent some time patiently talking her out of her fears, then they went to bed. When the lights were out she rolled into his arms and urged his body to take her, as if only the raw heat of lovemaking could melt her fears and forge new strength in her. He entered her swiftly but gently, and she reared up and caught her hands behind his neck, pulling him down to her and writhing her hips against his. She moved with violent need beneath him, her long nails raking his back and buttocks, pulling and urging him to climax. They came together in a long sinuous paroxysm of pleasure that seemed to hold them in its grasp for minutes on end.

Sated, they collapsed onto the sweat-soaked mattress. Dawn Palmer stayed in the protective circle of his arms and at last sleep carried them both into the night.

5

The next morning, Santillo and Weston were summoned to Lt. Hunt's office, where they met one of the representatives of the mayor's office, a young up-and-comer named Kramer who dressed like a disciple of *Gentleman's Quarterly* and sported a politician's smile: one that's so full of sincerity that you'd never suspect he was going to stab you in the back. He greeted Santillo with a nod and Weston with a firm handshake.

"I want to congratulate you on the way you handled yourself at the museum last night," Kramer told Weston. "A job well done, a real tribute to the department the way you saved the hakim."

"I'm not so sure he was worth the effort," Weston said. "But there were people at the museum who were."

"Not worth the effort?" Kramer blanched. "What do you mean?"

"I don't like dictators, even if they have been deposed," Weston said bluntly. "Especially ones that made a habit of killing off their countrymen while robbing them blind."

"I hope you keep your political views away from the press," Kramer said in a strangled voice. "The hakim is a guest in New York City."

"It's not a political opinion," Weston claimed, "it's just plain common sense. Guys who kill innocent people ought to be locked up: I don't care if he's a Bronx hood or an African hakim. He's a killer."

"Can it," Lt. Hunt snapped. "Mr. Kramer is not here to listen to our views on this hakim character."

"Correct," agreed Kramer, pulling himself together and getting his smile in operation again. "I want you to tell me, Detective Weston, how it happens that you were at the museum last night."

"My wife and I were on our way to the baroque music concert there."

"You don't strike me as a music-lover," Kramer scoffed. "I'm serious, I want to know the truth. Did you suspect that there would be an attack on the hakim, did you get a tip of some kind, a threatening message?"

"My wife wanted—"

"Or perhaps you suspected the hakim of something illegal and decided to keep an eye on him?"

"My wife wanted to go to the music concert... played on the original instruments," Weston added and Santillo nodded with interest, saying, "Do tell."

Kramer flushed, then turned to Lt. Hunt. "I hope you'll remember my request, lieutenant," he said coldly, then pushed past the two detectives and left.

"Is that music story on the up and up?" Lt. Hunt wanted to know. When Weston assured him it was, the lieutenant told his two cops: "This African hakim,

110

or whatever he is, has a few million bucks he's thinking of investing in our fair city, and the boys at City Hall would like to make sure he doesn't change his mind and take his money somewhere else. They need his money here badly. You know City Hall: they don't care if he got it pimping his grandchildren, they just want that investment. So they want to make his stay here as pleasant as possible, they especially don't want us to take it upon ourselves to try to protect him from this guy who's after him, this Yusef Ramad. Understood? Good." Lt. Hunt, drumming stubby fingers on the desk top a minute as he regarded his two detectives with a critical eye, said, "Any time the city is entertaining some V.I.P. we have to stay out of the guy's way, we have to walk on eggs around any V.I.P. Now in practical terms what this means is that if you guys want to question the hakim you have to go through channels. And you guys got one channel, and it's me. The mayor's go-fer who just walked out of here was a little pissed off that *I* had sent Christian over to question the hakim yesterday. I wish *I'd* known *I'd* done that, Weston," he concluded with dangerous sweetness.

"He was a lead," Weston replied. "One of his companions was seen talking to a victim and I figured—"

"I don't want to hear your figuring," Lt. Hunt fumed. "The next time you have to question an out-of-town V.I.P. like him, you go through me first. It seems Christian is about as diplomatic as you two are, and the hakim complained to the mayor." He gave a derisive snort, then turned directly to the subject of Matt Christian. "How's he working out?"

"Okay," Santillo shrugged.

"Where the hell is he anyway? I wanted to put some hot coals in that guy's pants."

"He's tailing a model named Dawn Palmer." Santillo told the lieutenant about the threatening photograph she'd received last night. "It looks like she's next on the killer's list, so we're tailing her round the clock."

"She moved in with you?" Lt. Hunt mused.

"Just until this thing blows over."

"Christian and Weston tail her all day, and you're on her tail all night, huh? Quite a setup for you, Santillo." Lt. Hunt shook his head in mock admiration, then asked: "Are you getting at all closer to the psycho behind these model killings?"

"The lab's turned up the usual reams of scientific jargon that translates into English as 'nothing.'"

"We'd better get something from somewhere, and fast. If another model gets the knife, the commissioner will hand our asses to us on a platter." Lt Hunt turned to Weston: "How about this sniper? Anything?"

"I'm still waiting for the lab report on the beret and his nest at the latest sniping."

"What the hell is taking them so long? Don't they realize this is an important case?"

"I'll give them a call and remind them," Weston promised.

Santillo and Weston spent the day reading police dossiers on dozens of people whose names had cropped up in the course of their investigations of the two cases. All they got for their trouble were tired eyes and sore butts.

At five o'clock they called it a day and headed for home, Weston for his house in Brooklyn, Santillo for lower Manhattan.

Santillo found Matt Christian in the café directly opposite his own apartment house, a cozy place run by an elephantine Italian woman who seemed to think of every customer as a close and dear relative, and showed them fawning concern every minute they spent in the place. She was hovering over a dour-looking Matt Christian when Santillo came in, and even this woman's vast patience seemed to have met its match in Christian. She gave Santillo an I-hope-your-friend-gets-better look, then wandered off to a couple in the corner.

"I wish that old cow would keep out of my hair," Christian declared loudly enough to be heard clear across the room.

"She's a good woman. She cares about people."

"Tell her to care about somebody who needs it," Christian snapped. "I don't. I like to be on my own."

"You like to work on your own, too, don't you?"

"What does that mean?"

"Wes called the lab to ask about the sniper reports. They told him that you've been picking up all the reports yourself."

"And you think that because I haven't repeated everything to you *ver batim* that I've been holding out on you." He laughed, one hard burst of sound, like a muffled backfire. "There's nothing in the reports, the lab gave us a big zero—no prints anywhere because the sniper wore gloves, no telltale hairs on the beret. Nothing. Read the reports yourself if you think I'm holding out on you—they're in the bottom drawer of the filing cabinet." He dismissesd the subject with a curt wave of his hand, then flipped open a notebook, and said: "Let's cut the crap! I got other things to do tonight. You want a complete rundown of Dawn Palmer's movements today?"

"Just the highlights."

Christian recited her movements in detail anyway: her agent's office, Germain's Studio One, dentist appointment, lunch at Bowman's Grotto, the Jenkins Studio, Broadway audition, cab home. He even gave the license number of the cab. Grinning meanly, he concluded: "She didn't have enough money for the cab fare so she took the car jockey into the lobby and paid up with some nooky."

"You've got a foul mouth, Christian."

"Try doing something about it, Santillo." He stood up, stretched. "I don't consider it a privilege to keep tabs on some whore just because the great Santillo is shacked up with her." And he was gone.

Before going upstairs to his apartment Santillo had a cup of coffee and waited until his anger at Christian had died down. Christian riled him; intentionally made cracks just to get his goat, like that lie about Dawn and the cabbie. Theirs was not a partnership made in heaven, that was for sure. He shook off thoughts of Christian and went up to the apartment, where he discovered Dawn in the little kitchen, concocting some meatless casserole.

"Soybean curd stew," she announced proudly.

It looked like something the dog had dragged in, and tasted like something the dog wouldn't waste his time dragging in.

"You shouldn't feel obligated to cook dinner," he insisted. Especially if it tastes like this one, he added in his thoughts.

"I don't feel obligated exactly. I enjoy it. But I have to show my appreciation for your taking me in like this..."

"I can think of other ways to show it..."

Apparently she could also, for she smiled and got up and walked over to Santillo, kissed his eyes shut, then unbuttoned his shirt and left a track of wet kisses across his chest. He pulled her down beside him on the couch. He undid the strap of her wraparound blouse, and parted the material. Her firm breasts glistened under a sheen of perspiration. He lowered his mouth to one smooth nipple and nibbled it hard. Her hands were busy between his legs caressing, teasing.

"Let's skip the foreplay tonight," she whispered urgently, as she rolled under him.

He thrust into her in one slow movement that made both of them gasp.

"Let me do the work," she offered, and immediately started moving her hips in gentle circles that started a warmth radiating through Santillo. Within a minute, he wanted to thrust hard and finish the exquisite torture, but she held him firm, and kept up the slow rhythm of her hips, and long minutes later she brought him to climax. As it pulsed through him, she came too, intensely, throwing her arms around and yelling like an attacking banshee. Santillo half-expected the neighbors to start pounding on the door to try to stop the murder going on in there.

Later, while Dawn Palmer was washing the dishes, Santillo took the garbage out to the trash room at the end of the hall. He added his garbage bag to the others, then started back to his apartment but stopped in the hall. An alarm bell was ringing in his head, something....

But he couldn't figure out what was bothering him. He stood there a moment, absolutely still, nagged by an uneasy feeling akin to sensing that you're being watched. But there was no one there.

Santillo went back to his apartment, but the uneasy feeling stayed with him. He went into the bedroom, tucked his .38 into his pants' waistband, exchanged his slippers for a pair of shoes, then went back out again.

"Where are you going?" Dawn asked.

"Back in a minute."

In the hall, Santillo paused, listening, hearing only the murmur of his neighbors' voices, the ever-present churn of traffic from the streets, nothing that reinforced his sense of foreboding. Maybe it was just his imagination. He walked slowly down the hall, retracing his path to the garbage room. In reproducing the actions he had taken earlier, he even went so far as to open the door as he had done before. And then he realized what had been nagging his unconscious mind. It wasn't something Santillo had seen or heard. It was a smell.

Inside the garbage room was the heavy odor of garbage—rotting vegetables and old cigarette ashes and wet papers—but intermingled with this was a lighter smell, a sweet odor Santillo had smelled once before—in the bathroom of the hotel suite where Melissa Martin had been murdered. The scented soap used by the killer of Melissa Martin. It was a strong, lingering odor, the kind that might remain in the air after a man had left. The killer could have been standing where Santillo was standing right now: the little room was not exactly a pleasant place from which to watch Santillo's apartment, but it offered a good view and was really the only place a person could wait without being observed. How long ago had the guy left?

Santillo walked to the elevators, pushed the button, but the elevator just stayed in the basement garage. Santillo went to the other end of the hall, then down a side corridor to the back stairs door.

He stepped out onto the landing and sniffed the air like a bloodhound seeking a scent. He felt like a damn fool. But he could also catch a waft of the soapy scent. He went down the stairs, at each floor stopping to take a look down the hall, but saw no one. On the ground floor, one floor above the basement garage, he paused, and looked down the stairwell. The stairwell light in the basement was not on, leaving a pit of darkness below. The only break in the darkness beneath him was the glowing bar of light beneath the door to the garage. That meant that the lights in the garage were turned on, with the stairway dark those lights would have the effect of spotlighting the door. A man coming from the darkness of the stairwell into the brightness of the garage would be temporarily blinded, making him an easy target for an attack. Like shooting one of those mechanical squirrels at a fairground gallery. And the elevator was out of operation, forcing a man to take the stairs.

Santillo backtracked to the ground floor landing, went out into the hall and walked to the elevators. The indicator over the door showed that the elevator car was still in the basement. In the wall near the floor, a metal lid covered the elevator's emergency controls. Santillo jimmied the lid off with a pocket knife, then pressed the door release. He was then able to push open the elevator doors and look into the shaft.

Two feet below floor level was the roof of the elevator car. Santillo gently stepped down onto the roof, knelt beside the roof hatch and began loosening the butterfly nuts that held the hatch covering in place. He quietly lifted the covering and slid it to one side so that he could see into the elevator car. The car itself was empty, but an old chair had been wedged between the doors to hold them open and keep the elevator out of service.

Santillo eased the metal covering off the opening, then lowered himself through the opening. He dropped quietly to the floor of the car, then put his eye to the edge of the half-open door. The elevator shaft was set in a big support column in the middle of the small garage. The elevator doors opened directly opposite the stairway door, which as Santillo had guessed, was brilliantly illuminated. One of the spotlights on a nearby pillar had been tilted to throw the stairway entrance into bright light, blinding and spotlighting any man coming down those stairs. It was a clever setup. The only question remaining was where was the man who had so carefully orchestrated this trap? Santillo could not see much of the garage from his position inside the elevator, but he knew the arrangement well enough: the only cover in the garage were the rows of cars parked along each of the side walls. The killer must be waiting there. Either side offered a good shooting blind, but the left side was better because the lights on that side of the garage were off. Santillo scanned the darkness between the only two cars he could see on that side. There was no one there.

He eased himself outside the elevator, and flattened himself on the ground against the concrete pillar beside the door. He crawled to one corner, put his eye to the edge and from here he could see the whole line of cars along the left wall. A dozen or so, with only two vacant slots. It was in the most distant of the vacant ones that Santillo saw the pale oval of a face, no more than a blur in the shadows, hanging immobile, like a small moon. Santillo eased back from the corner, then crawled around to the other side of the pillar, where he could get a better angle on the vacant slot where he'd seen the pale face. But this time when he put his eye to the corner he saw no pale oval, just unbroken darkness between the cars. He waited, scanning the line of cars, but saw no sign of the guy. The garage was silent as a cathedral.

Then a babble of voices spilled out of the stairway door, growing louder as a party of perhaps half a dozen people trooped down the stairs. A couple of men and women, the women doing some giggling, one of the men complaining about the elevator being out of operation. They would be coming through the door in less than a minute and it was just possible that the man lying in wait for Santillo would get nervous and shoot one of them. He might do it accidently, out of nervousness, or he might do it intentionally, just for kicks. With psychos like the model killer, you could never tell what he might do. Santillo didn't like the idea of showing himself, but he had no choice in the matter: he either showed himself or ran the risk of innocent people getting killed.

Santillo held off until a couple of seconds before the people appeared, then he broke cover, taking a couple of deliberately noisy steps and diving into the darkness between parked cars on the garage's right hand wall. He hit hard on the concrete, banging his head on a Jaguar's hubcap and his hip on a fender, but that was all the harm that was done: no slugs followed him into the row of cars.

He pivoted around and took a look at the far wall. Nothing but darkness lurking between the cars over there. Had he imagined the pale oval of a man's face, had it just been the after-image of a dark form burning the retina?

The six people were in the garage now and one of them came over and angrily removed the chair from the door of the elevator, then they all climbed into an ancient Ford. The Ford deposited a snake of exhaust across the garage as it drove up the ramp and out onto the street. As the Ford turned to the left Santillo saw something in the taillight reflection, a quick movement on the right. Another illusion? Or a man leaving the garage under cover of the Ford?

Santillo crossed the garage to the door and took a look outside. Moonlight turned the sidewalks to luminous beaches that edged the black river of the street. The sidewalks were crowded: young couples walking arm-in-arm; a pair of old women dragging shopping carts full of laundry to the laundromat on the corner; a troop of teenagers on their way to a movie; people gathered on the front stoops to complain of the heat; some kids running and yelling through a hydrant geyser. And above the street men and women leaned out of windows and watched the night air stir the heat around. A typical hot summer night in Santillo's neighborhood—nothing to indicate that a killer was prowling the streets.

Santillo tucked the snubnose .38 out of sight so as not to alarm anybody, then walked along the sidewalk, eyes prying into the darkness at every corner, but seeing no one who shouldn't be there. He stopped at the sagging stoop of one brownstone walkup where three guys in sleeveless undershirts were discussing the failure of the Yankees to beat Baltimore that afternoon.

"Anybody here see a man come out of the garage back there?" Santillo interrupted. Two of the guys shook their heads, but the third said:

"Blond hair, kind of a fast walker?"

"That's him," Santillo said, even though he hadn't seen the guy's head well enough to make out the hair color. It could have been blond; at any rate, it was a safe bet that the guy would be walking fast.

"Yeah, I saw him," the guy said, and pointed up the street with his beer. "That's funny... he was just a little ways up there... must have been walking faster than I thought. No! There he is!"

Santillo caught sight of a figure on the other side of the street, moving quickly between the evening strollers. The figure ducked into a café in the middle of the block. All Santillo could make out for sure was that the guy did have blond hair.

Santillo went to the café and stood looking in the window a while, but couldn't see the newcomer.

He went inside, where a harrassed waitress told him somebody had come inside but she didn't see where he'd gone.

"Maybe he turned around and went out again," she suggested, "or maybe he's in the can."

The door leading to the washrooms opened onto a hall that ran past the MEN's and LADIES'. At one end was the kitchen, at the other a fire door with a bar handle leading to the alley behind the café. Santillo checked both washrooms, came up empty, then pushed open the fire door. There was no one outside. In the alley Santillo saw the side door of a strip joint just swinging closed. The guy was like a phantom, always one step ahead, just vanishing when Santillo caught up.

Santillo went through the door of the strip joint and into a dark corridor that ended in a curtained doorway. He pulled back the curtain on a dimly lit room that was overheated with the warmth of too many people in too small a space. A dozen patrons were holding up the bar that ran along one wall; small tables were crammed together around a small curtainless raised platform that passed for the stage in a dump like this one. On stage a bored-looking woman with sagging breasts was going through the motions of taking her clothes off to the rhythm of scratchy strip music. The air was thick with the smell of stunted desire, and cigarette smoke hung in a pall over the sweating faces that were turned toward the stage. Santillo stayed close to the bar and let his eyes wander among those faces. Each one looked totally absorbed in the stage performance, where the stripper was now in the process of coyly taking off her G-string, and swinging into her finale.

All she now wore were stilletto heels, an appendicitis scar and her bored expression. She was standing at the lip of the stage, hands on hips, naked breasts glistening with sweat in the dim light; her legs moved farther and farther apart with each beat of the music until she was almost doing the splits, and then she suddenly dropped to her knees and bent over backward, dragging her hair from side to side on the stage floor, her hips swinging and lunging with the rising crescendo of the music. What she lacked in looks and enthusiasm, she more than made up for in acrobatic agility.

Santillo was looking over the patrons in the big gold-veined mirror behind the bar when he saw a shadow move in the dark entrance of a hall on the other side of the room. He turned around, and then a gunshot exploded in the hall and a slug nipped at Santillo's sleeve and splintered the mirror.

The club's patrons were frozen for one long moment in immobile silence by the gunshot; then some caught sight of Santillo moving across the room with his gun drawn and a bunch of men surged to their feet and made a run for the front door, cutting Santillo off from the gunman's exit. By the time Santillo had made it to the hall on the other side of the room, the hallway was empty. Santillo went through the first door he came to. Another corridor, this one leading to an area adjacent to the stage. As Santillo entered the hall, the lights all over the strip joint went out. The hallway was pitch dark.

Guiding himself with a hand against the wall, Santillo moved quickly along, listening for the sounds of movement. He heard the brushing of footsteps, then held stock still. A moment later a match flared in the darkness to the right and in the orange glow Santillo could see the naked breasts of the stripper. The woman peered nearsightedly at Santillo.

"What the hell's going on around here?"

"A man go by you?"

"A man . . . ? I don't know, sweetie, but somebody sure as hell did go past me a second ago. Nearly knocked me on my keyster." She stopped when she saw the weapon in Santillo's hand. "Cop? Shit, I didn't recognize you without my clothes on." When she saw that her little joke didn't bring a smile to Santillo's face she pointed a long red-tipped finger at a door. "He went through there, into the basement."

When the lights had been restored, Santillo opened the basement door, reached into the stairwell and threw the basement switch. A dozen wooden steps led to a dirt-floor cellar stacked high with cardboard cases of wine and beer bottles. But from the top of the stairs Santillo couldn't see much of the cellar without making an easy target of himself. Maybe there were faster ways of committing suicide than walking into a cellar after a killer with a gun, but offhand Santillo couldn't think of one.

"Is there another way out of the basement?" he asked the stripper.

"No. Even the windows are barred," she informed him. "Is there anything I can do to help?"

"Yeah. Bring me a small mirror from your dressing room."

Santillo strapped the mirror at an angle to the handle of a broom. He poked the broom down into the stairwell and looked the room over in the reflection. After five minutes of looking, Santillo went down the steps and confirmed that the basement was empty.

"Are you sure he went down here?" Santillo asked the stripper.

"Well, I heard the door open and close, and I guess I just assumed..."

As simple as that—opening and closing a door—and a false trail was left, enabling the killer to return to the front of the strip joint, and leave along with the other patrons, while Santillo wasted five minutes standing watch on an empty basement.

Five minutes was a lot of time to waste. If this guy was as bold as Santillo thought, five minutes was more than enough time for him to return to Santillo's apartment house.... Santillo was up the stairs and out the back door in seconds, running flat out down the alley and across the street, dodging a Chev and forcing a guy in a sleek Italian Mazeratti to stand on his brakes. Santillo took a short cut back, going down an alley, jumping over a fence at the back and cutting through a narrow plot of lawn, the way he had done as a kid in this same neighborhood. He emerged across from his building, crashed through the lobby and up the stairs. Every step of the way a little voice in his head was cursing him and calling him the biggest fool on God's asphalt footstool.

His apartment door was closed but unlocked. The living room was empty; Santillo pushed open the bedroom door. The unmade bed sheets were still in a rumple from their morning's lovemaking, but the room was empty of life. Santillo's heart sank. He checked the bathroom, and found it empty, too. He returned to the living room, picked up the phone, and was dialling police headquarters when the front door opened and Dawn Palmer walked into the living room. Her beautiful face was serene and untroubled as a child's.

"What've you been up to?" she asked.

"Checking on some things," he said calmly. "How about you?"

"Went out for some cigarettes," she replied. "This is a nice neighborhood you live in, Vince. Nice people. Kind of a family atmosphere. Very relaxing, in spite of this terrible heat."

"Yeah, very relaxing," Santillo agreed mopping his forehead dry. "For some people."

Weston was made restless by his lack of progress on the sniper case, so after dinner he got in his car and returned to Manhattan to take another look at the scenes of the previous three snipings. By picking up the feel of the snipers previous target areas, he thought he might be able to come up with some ideas on the next place of attack.

He visited the hotel linen closet overlooking Eighth Avenue; a tenement in Harlem, where the sniper had first struck; an empty office overlooking Amsterdam Avenue, near Needle Park. The three locations had one thing in common—they were full of prostitutes. That didn't tell Weston anything new. He felt more depressed than ever.

As he emerged from the building on Amsterdam Avenue he walked right into Jessica Newman, the salesclerk at the Fox-E, Enterprises, magazine store.

"You work long hours, Detective Weston," she said with a playful smile. "Or am I a suspect you've been following?"

"Are you guilty of something, Miss Newman?"

"Yeah. Lustful thoughts," she said. "And call me Jessica."

"What are you doing here tonight, Jessica?"

"Taking light exposure readings." She held up a light meter and a notebook into which she'd been recording the readings. "They're going to shoot some night street scenes here and wanted preliminary readings. You're just in time to give me a hand." She handed him the notebook and he wrote down the numbers she read to him.

"Have you remembered anything else about the man who bought those magazines?" Weston asked.

"I'm afraid not," she replied. "You're always thinking of business, aren't you?"

"It's the kind of work that makes you think about it."

She took the last reading then asked Weston if he'd like to join her for a drink. "I know a nice place that's not too far from here. Cozy and quiet. You can prime my memory with alcohol. Who knows what I might remember in the right mood."

They got into his Chevrolet and she gave him an address in Greenwich Village. As he drove, she sat in the corner and filled the air with the gauzy smoke of a sweet-smelling cigarette.

"You're married, aren't you?" she asked.

"Yeah."

"Love her?"

"You could say that."

"I just did, didn't I?"

The address she'd given him was a brownstone a few blocks north of the New York University campus.

The street was filled with similar brownstones, on both sides, and if there was a bar or café around it was well-hidden.

Nonetheless, she proclaimed: "Here we are." She slid across the seat until her thigh pressed against his. "My place is third floor rear. As promised: cozy and quiet." She opened the door herself and from the sidewalk bent down and talked to Weston through the open door: "I'm not looking for love, Weston, probably wouldn't know it if I found it. All I want is something to help me forget I'll wake up alone in the morning."

He followed her into the building. At the third floor landing she turned to face him, and he walked up into her arms. His mouth found hers, and he felt a tautness enter her and her hands gripped his arms tightly. He nibbled at the lobe of her ear, and felt her sigh riffle through his sideburns.

"Tsk-tsk!" A woman carrying a shopping bag and wearing a tent dress that looked big enough to conceal a team of circus midgets came out of one of the apartments and glowered at Weston and Jessica as though they were vandals. "Can't you find a more private place to kiss?" she huffed.

"I like to start out by kissing these places first," Weston told her. "I kiss the private ones later."

The woman gave a shocked gasp and hurried down the stairs, the boards shuddering with each thunderous step.

Jessica, laughing, led Weston to her own apartment, two small rooms with windows on a dingy courtyard that the sun never touched. Moonlight gilded the railing of a fire escape platform outside the window.

"A drink or some grass?" Jessica offered.

He chose the grass. He was in the mood, needed something that could alter his perception of things, something that could put the sniper case in a new perspective. Good grass could do that, and the stuff that Jessica had was good, Colombian Red. Three tokes and he was flying. But once he took off it wasn't the sniper he was thinking about, it was Jessica. He couldn't take his eyes off her.

She was wearing a flower-patterned skirt and a white peasant blouse, beneath which her taut breasts moved freely. She leaned back beside him on the couch and he reached out and trailed a hand down the downy hairs of her arm. She shivered and gooseflesh rose on the smooth skin. The dark of her nipples condensed to twin fingers that poked gently at the thin fabric of her blouse.

She moved into his embrace, opened her mouth to his, and their probing tongues met, exchanging heat. He moved a hand across her ruffled blouse and gently touched her breast, and her hard nipple moved against his fingers. Sliding his hand into the blouse, he stroked the downward slope of her breast and heard the rhythm of her breathing change.

Warm breath in his ear: "Maybe it's time for those private places you talked about..."

He parted her blouse and licked at the warm salty sweat dewing on her breasts. He sucked a hard nipple into his mouth, tongued it and felt it get harder, plied it gently with his teeth, while he loosened her skirt and began to pull it down. When her skirt was a puddle of cloth clinging to one ankle, he gently pushed her legs apart, and started stepping kisses down across her stomach.

"No ... no ..." she said, but her body denied the protest: her hips pressed upward to meet him, and her hands on the back of his head kept holding his mouth down there.

When he knew she was ready for him, he started to raise his head, but she moaned as though in pain and firmly held his head where it was. So he thought, what the hell, why not, and he kept at it with his tongue, and her locked fingers got more and more rigid in his hair, and when she came she almost pulled his hair out by the roots, her voice raised in a wailing cry, her throbbing body bouncing and shuddering as though she'd just taken a killing jolt of electricity. She lay a while, panting, recovering slowly, then slid off the couch to where Weston was kneeling on the carpet.

"Tit for tat," she murmured, and she pulled his belt loose and then unzipped him.

He lay back, as her stroking fingers drifted across his lower stomach, and then slid into his shorts. Her fingers balked at the hardness of him, then moved again, massaging and tugging his pants below his hips. She knelt above him, staring down, then, with a smile, lowered her head and captured him with her warm eager mouth. Up and down, up and down. She moaned, and the vibration coursed straight through him and seemed to set his nerves quivering. Up and down, up and down, her hands holding his surging hips down so that she could totally control the rhythm. Her tongue warm and wonderful on him.

Moments passed. The pleasure—with the grass heightening every sensuous detail—was overwhelmingly intense, and for a long time Weston was so caught up he almost forgot to breathe. Up and down, up and down, then Jessica's mouth released him. He pushed her back onto the floor and rolled on top of her. Her hands pulled his hips and he was in her with one lunge, and thrusting with urgency. Within seconds she came again, writhing under him, and her twisting movements triggered him and suddenly all the heat in his body exploded out of him. Her hungry body drained him dry. Minutes passed before either of them felt like speaking.

"This damn floor is breaking my back," Jessica said.

"Said with a true flare for romance," he said.

They moved to the bedroom, where they again made love. They started on the large water bed, but again—somehow forced by the repositionings that passion dictates—they ended up on the floor in a tangle of bedclothes.

At 10:30 P.M. Weston decided to leave. He followed his trail of discarded clothes out to the living room, where he got dressed in darkness. Jessica stayed in the bedroom a moment, then came to the door wrapped in a bedsheet, her long hair falling in brown waves around her shoulders.

"Thanks," she said with a wry grin, "I needed that."

Weston didn't know what to say, but he gave her a tender smile. He was glad he did because it was the last thing she ever saw; she would not have to worry about waking up alone in the morning, she would not have to worry about anything, ever.

There was not even a breath of sound as warning. One moment she was standing there with a sad smile on her lips, the next moment she was spun into a pirouette by the bullet, blood leaping from her torn back. A second bullet hit her just as she stopped spinning, nearly taking off her left shoulder. It hit her so hard she was shoved right past Weston and into a bookcase that came tumbling down on top of her. The guy who was shooting from the bedroom window was taking no chances: not only was he using a powerful handgun, probably a .357 Magnum, he was also using dum-dums that fragmented on contact, like grenades, sending probing metal fingers through the victim's pliant flesh.

Weston dived for cover, rolled across the carpet and came up on his knees next to the couch. He could see a dark form on the fire escape landing outside the bedroom window, then a muzzle flash as the guy sent yet another bullet into the dead woman. Weston put a .38 slug right through the middle of the open window but he was a split-second late, the form had already retreated out of sight.

Weston had no doubt it was the sniper out there, eliminating Jessica because she might remember enough about him to put Weston on his trail. She hadn't, of course, her murder had been pointless, but then all of the others were pointless, too. Jessica was lying still now, a disfigured corpse in a widening stain of blood. The only thing Weston could do to help her now was to catch her killer.

Weston scooted along the couch then dived through the bedroom doorway to the window. He saw the dark form of the sniper moving up the fire-escape ladder to the roof. Weston sent a bullet chasing after the guy, but it clanged off the metal and whined off into the night. The guy was over the parapet and gone a second later. Weston climbed out the window and clambered up the ladder. He went up two stories, then stopped on the landing just below the parapet. There, crouched low beneath the parapet, he waited a moment. He couldn't hear the sniper running. That might mean that the sniper was gone. Or it might not.

Weston pulled off his suit jacket, then, holding it by the collar, he tossed it straight up and a little to the right: to an anxious man who was expecting a target to appear, the jacket looked enough like a man's rising torso to tighten the trigger finger. And sure enough, the quiet "pfft-pfft" of a silenced gun was followed by the jacket jumping as two slugs nipped at it like angry bees. The shots came from behind a pigeon coop in the middle of the roof. Weston fired a slug right into the coop. A corner of the cage shattered, and a wire mesh door popped open, releasing the speckled fluttering of the birds as they leaped to freedom, squawking, feathers drifting in the air like snow.

Weston used the commotion as cover, and he vaulted the parapet, and scrambled behind a chimney stack. The sniper was on the move again, racing across the roof to the far parapet. He hit the parapet on the run, took one step up and leapt across to the next roof, which, unlike this one, was not flat, but steeply canted. His momentum carried him a ways up the sloping roof, he reached out both hands and grabbed the peak and hauled himself over to the other side.

Weston was right behind, but had more momentum and no trouble running right up the side of the roof. The sniper was on his way down the other side, jumping across the gap between buildings to the next roof. It was a bigger gap to jump this time, but he made it easily and started up the canted roof. Weston followed, landed on the roof running and was going hard up the slope when he saw that the sniper hadn't yet made the peak: he had come to a stop a few feet from the top, and his hands seemed to be slipping on the grainy shingles. He started a slow backslide. Weston moved out of the sniper's path, got his balance on the sloping roof, and stood up. The sniper was just about parallel with Weston now. His descent had gradually slowed to a stop. Weston pulled out his .38 and held it on the man.

The sniper moved slowly, carefully, as though to secure himself in his precarious perch. At least that's how it looked to Weston. But the slow, careful movement of his body was turned to a lethal one in the blinking of an eye: the sniper's leg leapt at Weston, long and hard and sure as a thrust saber and suddenly Weston's hand was aching and the .38 was angling out and down into the dark chasm between buildings. The guy was quick as a cobra and just as deadly: his leg kicked out again and Weston's stomach caved under the powerful thrust of his foot. The next thing Weston knew he was flat on his back, rolling down the roof toward the edge.

Weston flung out his arms and legs and that broke his roll, but now he was sliding sideways off the roof. His splayed fingers dug into the asphalt, but they did nothing to stop his descent. Then one leg and arm were over the edge, and he was beyond the last point of return.

He hooked a hand in the eaves trough, then as his momentum carried him off the roof he grabbed the trough with his other hand. His body swung off, and he was left hanging from the eaves trough. He could feel the dry muck in the trough oozing between his straining fingers. He hung there for a moment, and tried to shake off the welling nausea he felt where the guy had kicked him in the stomach. He was caught between a rock and a hard place: the sniper above, and a four story drop to concrete below. If the sniper took up running again and just left Weston to fall, then with a bit of luck Weston might be able to haul himself up onto the roof again before his hands gave out. But the sniper didn't retreat. He wasn't going to leave Weston's fall to chance, he was moving down the roof to crush Weston's fingers underfoot.

At the corner of the building a drainspout emerged from the eaves and snaked down the brick. It would be possible for Weston to descend that drainspout, but that corner of the building was some thirty feet off, and Weston hadn't the time to get over there before the sniper reached him. He didn't have much time at all: in a few seconds the sniper would be at the roof edge, grinding his heels against Weston's already weakening hands.

There was one hope, a slim one, but the only one Weston had: a couple of feet to the left was a frame window looking out into this space between buildings. Weston moved his hands along the eaves, inch by painful inch, until he was in line with the window. The eaves overhung the building by nearly four feet, so the window couldn't be reached easily. Weston started swinging his feet toward the window, and then back, building up momentum like a trapeze aerialist getting ready for a leap. At the outward peak of his swing he looked up and saw the dark figure of the sniper looming on the roof's edge, a stocky man with a black ski mask pulled over his face, his eyes and mouth dark holes in the dark material of the mask. Weston estimated he had time for one more swing before the sniper reached him. He was wrong.

The sniper unleashed one of his lethal kicks during Weston's next backswing, and pain scalded his hand, boiling up his arm to the elbow. The kick would have broken his fingers, and easily knocked him loose of the eaves, but the kick did not make clean contact: the flimsy eaves trough just then gave way a few inches under Weston's weight and saved him from direct impact. Weston's legs swung back toward the window and this time as they did he let go of the eaves trough, and he swung free, angling right across into the window.

As his feet crashed through the glass, he wrapped his arms around his head for protection, and he went through the window in a dazzling flurry of exploding glass that cascaded into the room with him like a luminous mist. Weston crashed down amid the glass, took a couple of stumbling steps as his weight carried him across the room and dropped him onto a large double bed.

On the other side of the room a brunette wearing a robe over a black negligée turned from her dressing table mirror, calmly pausing in the brushing of her hair as though Weston's entrance were standard practice on hot summer nights. She cocked an eyebrow.

"Is this something new in voyeurism?" she asked. "Three-D?"

Weston got to his feet and took a couple of seconds to take inventory of his bruised body: his face was scratched from the window pane, his stomach ached where the sniper had kicked him. His left hand hurt, too, but he could flex the fingers and even make a fist if he put his mind to it. But it hurt enough so that he would save it for an emergency. And he could see one taking shape already: the woman whose bedroom he had just crash-landed in was still facing him with icy calm, but now her hands held a pearl-handled automatic instead of the hairbrush. Her voice was as icy as her face:

"I advised you to stay right where you are. If you think I have any qualms about using this gun, then think again. And don't kid yourself that I'm not accurate enough to drop you where you stand."

"I'm a cop," Weston informed her. "I'll show you my i.d.—"

"Hold your hands in front of you, palms up," she commanded.

"I'm a cop," he repeated. "I was chasing a man—"

"Did you see him fly in through my window?" she snapped.

"That was my own idea," he admitted.

"Well, I've got an idea of my own. Let's wait right here while I call your friends at headquarters."

Cops rub elbows with death every day on the job, and so it's only natural that they should give a lot of thought to their own dying. They know they'll have to do it some day. It would be nice to meet death in old age, but there's always the chance you won't make it to old age, and if you have to die young, it's best to do it heroically, perhaps saving another person's life in the process. The worst fear of every cop is to get killed through some silly screw-up like this one, dying at the hands of an honest citizen who thinks she's ridding the city of a crook. No cop wants to be remembered as the guy who got killed when he sought refuge in a woman's bedroom, and so there was a strong temptation to let this woman have her way rather than run the risk of getting shot.

But a killer was getting away—Weston could hear the sniper moving across the roof now—and all Weston had to do was think of Jessica's brutal murder to know that he would have to take a chance.

"I'm going after the guy on the roof," he said, and without giving her any time to answer he turned and walked out of the room, not taking a breath until he was in the hall with the door closed behind him.

Weston got onto the roof through a dormer window in the attic. He saw the sniper three roofs away, descending a fire escape into the alley. Weston ran down to the back door of this building and got into the alley in time to hear the roar of an engine from the other end of the alley. Taillights burned red, then disappeared around the corner. Weston ran the length of the alley, but when he turned the corner the street was empty.

He cursed himself angrily, and then, depressed and frustrated, headed back to Jessica's apartment, where the dead woman waited in silent reminder of his failure.

6

Jane Turner tapped her long fingernails on the door marked 1527 and immediately Mitch Roundtree opened it, and stood grinning at her, as though he had been waiting anxiously for her to arrive. She met his smile with one of her own, then stepped into the hotel room and frowned at the shabby furniture that crowded the dusty little room.

"This isn't the kind of place I'd expect a designer of Lancia's reputation to choose," she said.

"That finally occurred to you, did it?"

She glanced at him, and now she could see something else in the smooth smile, a jagged edge of mocking, and she knew in an instant that there were no Lancia originals hanging in these closets, wondered whatever had made her think there could have been. There was nothing in these closets but dust and the dry husks of dead moths.

"What's the idea?" she demanded.

"The idea is a little—fun."

"Very little, judging from your attempt at a performance last month," she commented acidly. "You couldn't get it up with a derrick."

"This time we're going to have a different kind of fun." He hit her in the face and her head bounced off the wall, his signet ring leaving a welt glowing on her flushed cheek.

"Jesus," she said, dazed, and took a step back as he moved closer. "Jesus."

"He's not in today." He slapped her with the back of his hand and she staggered back until the bed caught her in the back of the knees, and she sat down.

He grabbed the front of her dress in his fist, and yanked down, ripping the dress from bust to hem. She raised her voice in protest, but his lashing fist quelled her cries. She instinctively brought her hands up to cover her breasts. He slapped her hands aside, then hooked his fingers in her bra and ripped it off her. He pulled off her panties the same way, tossing the tattered garments to the floor.

"We're going to have some visitors," he announced with a mean smile. "They're going to have the fun and you're going to oblige them. You cause so much as one minute's trouble and it'll be the last trouble you cause anybody. You get what I mean?"

She nodded. She got it all right, it was clear as spring water: three models had been slain in recent weeks, and if she did not watch her step she might become the fourth. She felt her heart beating in her throat, but she forced a smile to her lips and said, "Sure, Mitch. I'm not going to give you any trouble."

"You're damn right you're not."

"I mean, it's not like I'm a virgin or something."

"You can say that again, bitch." He was pacing near the foot of the bed, moving with the compressed strides of an agitated jungle cat. Sweat stained the front of his shirt, rolled down across the wrinkled brow. "You're damn right."

"I've had to put out for men before when I didn't want to—you can't get jobs in this racket without doing that. I guess, this won't really be any different."

"Maybe just a little different," he said quietly.

There was no missing the restrained glee in the cold voice. It made one thing obvious enough: she could be obliging as hell, and it wouldn't get her out of this room alive; when he was through with her, she'd be as dead as Melissa Martin and the others.

As Mitch Roundtree paced, he occasionally took his eyes off Jane Turner to look at his watch, and when he did that Jane sneaked glances around the room, looking for a way out. The door was locked with a bolt and a chain, and she'd need a lot of time to unlock them. The only other exit was a sash window near the bed she was sitting on. It stood open, letting warm air billow the chintz curtains. Eight floors down was the roof of the adjoining building, its tar gleaming like liquid in the hot sunlight. If she could get out the window she could move along the ledge to the fire escape that zigzagged its way down the wall. She thought about the long fall to the roof, and her mouth went dry as desert sand, but then she thought about staying here with Mitch Roundtree and she made her voice work around the dryness:

"When are they getting here, Mitch, these 'visitors'?"

"They'll be here, don't worry." But he cast another worried glance at his wristwatch.

"What I mean is, if they're going to be late maybe the two of us could . . ." She watched his desire complete the sentence in his hot eyes.

"With me?" Roundtree sneered. "The guy who can't get it up with a derrick?"

"We could try using some other means..." She moved her legs fractionally apart, and let the corner of the sheet that she'd been holding in front of her breasts slide slowly away.

The tip of his tongue licked his dry lips, and he took a step nearer to her, then stopped.

Closer, you bastard, she thought, and gently repositioned her legs a bit farther apart.

He moved like an automaton to stand in front of her, his body rigid as a frozen board. Desire and fear of his own failure mixed together in him, turning him solid, like cement and water turning to concrete on contact.

She remained sitting on the bed. She reached out and touched his chest. She let her hands move down to his pants, unzipped his fly. She snugged her head against his stomach and cooed as though she were having the time of her life; all the while she was doing it, stomach bile rose in her throat, making her sick at merely touching him. She pulled his pants down, letting them fall to the floor around his feet. She tugged his shorts down around his knees.

Let him try to race with me now, she thought.

He didn't take his glance off her. It was as though he were trying to brand her with his hot eyes.

"Close your eyes," she suggested, "relax, close your eyes and imagine..."

He closed his eyes. While her left hand caressed the taut muscles of his chest, her right moved to the bedside night table and her fingers found the base of the lamp. It was old-fashioned and heavy, but she found the strength to heft it. She swung the bulky lamp up at his head with one hand and the heavy base clipped him on the temple. He tried to step away, but he tripped over his pants and fell sideways on the bed. She hoisted the lamp with both hands, and heaved it at his head, but he brought up an arm to shield himself, and the lamp cracked against his elbow. He let out a yelp, and rolled off the bed.

She climbed onto the window sill and then on hands and knees scuttled out the window and onto the ledge. She teetered in the hot afternoon, clinging to the narrow concrete ledge. She moved along it, feeling the sandpaper-scrape on her knees. She was surprised to feel tears on her face, and realized only now how great an ache was working inside her. She was within inches of reaching the fire escape landing when she felt Mitch Roundtree's hand grab her ankle, and pull. She fell off balance and the ledge seemed to slide out from under her, and for one brief moment she was looking straight down to the roof below, eight stories into an inviting black pool.

In sheer panic she stretched her arms for the railing of the fire escape, and her sweating hands grabbed, slipped, and then held. She tried to kick her legs free of Mitch Roundtree's hands, but he held them tight, and pulled hard in an effort to tug her loose from the railing. But she held.

She wanted to laugh. Her life was at stake and fear was alive in her, yet she felt an overwhelming urge to laugh at the absurd situation she found herself in, like something from an obscene comic operetta: stark naked, she was suspended like a human rope between the window and the fire escape by a man with his pants around his knees. It was ludicrous. No life should end like this, especially not hers, she wasn't meant for this, she was the star of her own life, not a bit character that was expendable.

The absurdity brought her fury to a boil, and with a shout of anger she pulled with all her might, and her legs pulled out of Mitch Roundtree's grasp, and swung free. But she had not reckoned on the pull of her own weight, and her arms were too tired to support her now, her hands too slick with sweat, and in the duration of a heartbeat she knew she was going to die, and in that blinding moment of recognition as the railing slipped out of her gasp, she felt other things slipping, too, the hopes, dreams, fears, loves, the needs that had been her life. She opened her eyes to the pool of black that leapt up from below and filled her entire body, engulfing her ...

"Bitch," was Mitch Roundtree's epitaph for the falling woman. "Bitch, bitch ...." He kept repeating the word in a low angry monotone as he went around the hotel room removing all traces of his presence here. He carried her torn clothes and purse down to the basement, tossed them in a plastic garbage bag waiting for pick up, then went up to the ground floor and passed through the lobby.

He wanted to get out of the neighborhood fast, before the cops arrived, but he had to wait around to head off his afternoon's client. He put on his sunglasses, and paced the sidewalk, tension growing in him like a spring coiling. It seemed he'd had nothing but bad luck lately: first of all nearly getting caught by the cop Santillo. Santillo had neatly sidestepped a perfect trap in the basement garage and only

Mitch Roundtree's paranoic sense of caution had enabled him to get away with his life. Trying to kill the cop was a silly luxury, a bit of self-indulgence that Roundtree should have denied himself. Why take a foolish risk going after the cop, when it was Dawn Palmer who was the real source of his problems? Yes, Dawn Palmer was the one he should go after....

The silver Cadillac limousine glided silently to the curb, and the man called Farah got out of the front seat to meet Roundtree.

"I thought the hakim and I were to meet you in the hotel room," Farah said.

"There's been an—accident. I'm afraid we'll have to call off today's session."

"That's a great disappointment. The hakim was looking forward..." Farah opened the back door and Roundtree got in next to the hakim Abdul Abidi.

"Most disappointing," the hakim said when Roundtree had broken the news. Then: "You promised me a beautiful woman..."

"You'll have one."

"Can you arrange something for the coming week?"

"Yes. What day?"

"I will call you later to let you know the precise day I will require her."

Roundtree got out of the limo and took a cab back to the Jenkins Studio for an afternoon session wherein he took pictures for a pantyhose ad. Forty-five minutes of squinting through a lense at nyloned legs crossing and uncrossing, bending and straightening, then another forty-five in the darkroom.

He felt irritated because of the botch-up at the hotel. Not because Jane Turner had died, but because she had died before he'd got a chance to use his knife. Her death had been unconsummated, and he felt a weakness bordering on vertigo come over him at his disappointing loss. Fatigued and frustrated, he was resting in a beanbag chair in the studio when Dawn Palmer started posing for another photographer.

The bitch, he thought, and then decided that when the hakim settled on a day, that would be Dawn's day, that would be the day she would meet his knife. His spirits rose in anticipation, and suddenly he felt rested, revitalized.

When Dawn Palmer had finished her session, Roundtree followed her to the changing room, and stood around outside the open door. She noticed him watching her, and she stepped behind the seldom-used changing screen to get out of her costume and put on street clothes.

Roundtree went into the dressing room, and their eyes met over the top of the screen.

"Hi, Mitch," she said, pleasantly enough. She'd been in a good mood since meeting Santillo. The photograph I left in her apartment didn't scare her nearly enough, he thought.

It was a little soon for him to be setting her up, but he would do it anyway. He ached to have her, to make her his forever as only the knife can do. However, she was a shrewd woman and wary, so he'd have to make his trap perfect for her.

"Dawn," he said in his best business voice, "you and I are both professionals."

"Yes...?"

"What I mean is this: we both know that you don't like me. And let's face it, you've turned me down so many times, I'm not wild about you either." He showed her a smile to prove there was no ill-will. "But—and this is the key thing—we're professionals, good ones, and we're not going to let our differences interfer with our work, not going to let it stand in the way of our working together—if it's to our mutual benefit."

Dressed, she stepped out from behind the screen and asked, "Where is this leading, Mitch?"

"To a job that might be the one break we both could use."

"What is it?"

He made a show of looking around for eavesdroppers, then lowered his voice as if to guarantee secrecy: "I've been asked to take some pics for a top designer, using the best model I know. Namely you. If we click on this job the way I think we can, then"—he snapped his fingers and raised his forefinger like a rocket taking off—"the sky's the limit."

He knew she was interested by the way she lowered her voice when she asked: "What job is this?"

"I'll get to that," he said, "but first I want to make sure that you don't breathe a word about it to anybody."

"Okay."

"Not even to your boyfriend the cop," he warned. "This has got to be between the three of us: you, me and—Signon Lancia."

"Lancia? You're joking."

"Just be glad I'm not. He's got a knockout Fall design that he wants some pics for."

"I'll do it!"

"Not so fast. I am serious about the secrecy. Lancia

is pulling a stunt this year: he's introducing a style that is completely different from every other designer's. He's that kind of showman—and he doesn't want word leaked. While all the other designers are creating stuff along the same basic themes, Lancia is taking an entirely new approach. But he can only do that if it's kept quiet. You know how everybody and his mother is out to steal ideas in this business. If I find out after we do the session that you let anybody know about it—then I'll put a match to the negatives, and reshoot the line with another model."

"You wouldn't!"

"Guess again. Lancia's trusting me to do this on the q.t., so he can really spring one on the competition. If I can't guarantee that secrecy I'm not even going to touch the job. You can understand that." She did, and she agreed to do as he asked. "I'll rent a studio, and we'll meet there some day next week to shoot. I'll let you know when and where later."

"Fine. I promise to be in top form, Mitch. We'll kill them!"

"Yes," Mitch Roundtree said with a grin, "it'll be a killer of a session!"

7

The weekend passed in a blur of heat, and the next week showed no signs of letup. For five days the blazing sun seemed never to leave the sky, hanging in the pale blue infinity it unleashed its burning rays, its relentless light. And at night, the moon took its place and seemed to radiate the same ancient heat. The sidewalks radiated heat up through the soles of shoes and people felt trapped in hell itself. As the city sweltered, the last reluctant inhibitions melted away, and frazzled men and women felt their nerves get rawer and rawer like tender skin sunburned to a lobster red. What little wind there was just pushed the heat in deeper and ancient madness bubbled up to the surface of the mind.

In Morningside Heights, a man came home to a bad dinner so he murdered his wife, and his neighbors across the hall before he shot himself. A woman complained that her butcher was pressing the meat scales with his thumb, and when the butcher denied it she grabbed a cleaver and took off his thumb. Two cars bumped each other in a parking lot in Greenwich Village. The drivers fought, first verbally, and then by ramming each other's cars. Then they started in on other cars in the lot, and other incensed drivers joined in, turning the whole parking lot and part of three streets into a vast destruction derby. But the heat did not let up.

On Wednesday morning while Weston was taking his turn at keeping an eye on Dawn Palmer, Santillo and Matt Christian met in Lt. Hunt's office to discuss the progress of their two cases.

"We can sum it up in two words," Matt Christian said: "No progress."

"What about the latest model's death, this Jane Turner? Anything there?"

"No one knew why she went to the hotel, or who she was going to meet," Santillo answered. "The best guess is that she met the guy and got wise to him. They probably had a fight and she fell or was pushed out the window. As usual, no witnesses."

"The only reason you guys still have your jobs right now," Lt. Hunt told them, "is because the media didn't tumble to the fact that she was a victim of the killer. 'Accidental death,' we told 'em, and they swallowed it. But if they get wise to what happened, or if another model dies . . . ." He let them finish the unpleasant thought for themselves. "We looked good on that one, I must say," he went on bitterly. "Twenty-four hour a day surveillance on this Dawn Palmer woman, and the killer goes after another model. Santillo. You think he's still going to make a play for her?"

"I think so," he answered. "The guy's obsessed."

"I think we've scared him off," Matt Christian interjected. "He's not going to make a play for her now. We're just wasting manpower keeping a tail on her."

"The killer's threat—" Santillo started, but Matt Christian cut him off.

"You're not looking at this thing objectively. You've got the hots for this piece of ass and it's distorting your judgment. So what if she's hot stuff in the rack? That doesn't mean this killer's going to make a play for her."

Santillo turned to face Christian and the latter stepped back as though bracing himself for an attack.

Lt. Hunt snapped: "What the hell's got into you two? Don't we have enough trouble with crooks trying to kill us cops, now we're trying to kill each other?" He jabbed a stubby finger like a gun barrel at Matt Christian. "I don't know what's chewing on your balls, mister, but if you can't handle it better than you've been doing today, I'll see to it that you're spending the rest of your tour of duty with me pushing pencils. Get it?"

"Yes, sir," he answered sullenly.

"Good. Now let's hear what you've come up with on this sniper."

"The lab reports haven't given us a thing to work on," Christian complained. "The beret, the cigarettes, the magazine he left behind: they all add up to a big fat zero."

Lt. Hunt frowned and shook his head in disgust, then dismissed the two detectives:

"Get out of here, both of you, and get your asses in gear while they are still intact."

Santillo and Christian spent the afternoon poring over surveillance and lab reports, the summaries of interviews with witnesses and non-witnesses, and by four P.M. they were right where they were that morning. Only now they were more tired and—if possible—even more irritable. Matt Christian left to pick up the surveillance on Dawn Palmer, and half an hour later Weston dragged himself in, drooped into a chair like a flower wilting.

"Christ, is it hot," he murmured.

"Thanks for that bit of news, Weston," snapped Santillo, then he went on with bitter sarcasm: "You're a real detective, you are. Everybody on the street is sweating like pigs in a steambath. The mercury is breaking every thermometer in town, and with only those two slender clues, the great detective figures out that it's hot! You know, maybe you ought to get a job where you could put this talent for deducing and stating the obvious to good use. You could become a talk show host, or go into politics."

Weston just stared at this outburst, too amazed and too tired to react hostilely. After a moment he stood up, walked outside, closed the door, then came back inside the office, dragged himself over to the same chair and sat in it with all the energy he had shown before.

"Christ, is it hot," he murmured.

Santillo looked at him a long time, the anger draining out of his face, as a slow smile sneaked on. He laughed.

"Sorry, Wes," he said. "I just spent the whole afternoon cooped up in here with Christian and—"

"Enough said," Weston interrupted. "You would have been excused if you'd slit my throat when I came in."

Weston brought in a couple cups of coffee to give them something different to complain about, then decided to go over the reports of the previous snipings for the n-th time. He had to move his chair in order to pull open the bottom file drawer. He stacked the reports on his desk, turned to close the drawer, and paused, staring at the drawer.

"What's wrong?" Santillo asked.

"What's this?" Weston was pointing to the edge of the drawer, where there was a tuft of something gray-white clinging to the edge.

"Looks like a feather...."

Weston pulled it off and held it up to the light. That's what it was, a feather. Just a feather. But the way Weston looked at it told his partner that there was something important about it, and Santillo waited patiently until Weston spoke:

"A pigeon feather maybe?" Weston hypothesized. "It looks like there's a bit of roofing tar stuck to it."

"Meaning that it probably came from your chase with the sniper a few days ago. It must have stuck to your shoe and come off here."

"I don't put my feet up on the file drawers."

"Christian's shoe then," Santillo guessed. "He probably went up to take a look at the scene and it stuck to him then."

"He told me he did not visit the scene."

"He lied, in other words ... he's been putting more time in on the sniper case than he tells us about...."

"And maybe he's learning some things he doesn't tell us about."

It happened more often than a person would suspect: a cop would hold out important information from his colleagues, either out of sheer malice to make them look stupid, or—if he was ambitious—so that he could solve the case himself. A cop's reputation was made not on *how* he solved crimes, but on *which* crimes he solved. Solving a burglary and murder with the most brilliant deductions this side of Sherlock Holmes won't help your career one iota if the crime isn't well-known, but solve a poodle-napping that is in the public eye—even if you solve it by dumb luck—and your career gets a boost. The temptation for Matt Christian was obvious: he comes into C.A.T. as an outsider, and solves a big murder case entirely on his own—his career is made.

"He also told us there was nothing in the lab reports on the beret and cigarettes." Santillo dialled the lab and asked about the reports.

"We've given all of them to C.A.T.," the lab technician said. "As I recall a guy named Christopher picked them up."

"Christian."

"That's the guy. He's been getting them all. Isn't he with your detail?"

"Yeah, but we lost the report and—"

"I can't give you our copy," the lab technician asserted. "And we can't have the secretary retype one without a requisition—"

"We don't need another copy, we just want to know what's in the report. Would you mind getting your copy and reading the—"

"As a matter of fact I do mind," he snapped. "The copies are in Documentation, and I don't have time to troop all over the place just to make up for the inefficiency of your detail. We're hip deep in—"

Santillo let him complain to the dial tone.

"What'd you get?" Weston asked.

"A bad time and a bucket of red tape. Let's go over to the Documentations section ourselves."

The police laboratories occupied one of the two sub-basements, but the lab's Documentation Department was on the third floor which it shared with the N.Y.P.D. computer. The overworked clerk got the reports for Santillo and Weston without a word of complaint. It took a while to plow through the scientific jargon. But when they did, they came up with some important facts: a brown hair in the beret indicated the sniper used a medicated shampoo; a partial fingerprint; deposits of Chapstick on the cigarette butts; the ink used to mark up *Hot Fox* was a distinctive one sold in only a few stores in the city. It added up to a lot more than the "nothing" Matt Christian had claimed he'd found in the reports.

"The bastard's been holding out on us," said Santillo. "He wants the collar for himself."

Both cops were angry: not because they wanted any share of the glory in capturing the sniper, but simply because three men could do the leg work of following up clues a lot faster than one man, and that meant the sniper would be off the streets that much faster.

"The question is," added Weston, "what else is he holding out on us?"

"Let's talk to him and find out."

Each of the detectives assigned to C.A.T. carried pageboy beepers so they could be reached twenty-four hours a day. Weston dialled the special telephone number that triggered Christian's pageboy, but twenty minutes passed and there was no return call from Christian.

"Let's take a look at his apartment," suggested Santillo.

The address they got from personnel was of a

ground floor apartment in a walkup just south of Houston Street in the Bowery. When Santillo and Weston pulled their Plymouth to the curb in front of the place, there were a couple of bums on the stoop next door playing tug-of-war with a wine bottle in a paper sack. A grizzled old guy in last year's rags was rummaging through a garbage can at the curb. The heated air was weighted with the stench of garbage and sewage. It was not the sort of neighborhood an ambitious cop would normally choose to call home.

Glued across the paneling of the front door were big gilt-edged letters: TEMPLE OF CHRISTIAN SALVATION. Pasted to the wall all around the doorbell were hand-written quotes from the Bible, warning sinners to repent, exhorting them to turn away from lust and greed.

"This can't be the right place," Weston mumbled, but he pushed the button anyway.

A moment later the door was opened by an enormous woman wearing a long black gown that hung in loose folds like a priest's robe, a crucifix hung between her pendulous breasts. Her pale face was engulfed by long waves of black hair that tumbled beyond her shoulders and got lost in the folds of her dress.

"Come in, come in," she invited, and let them into a hallway whose walls were covered with photographic reproductions of paintings of Jesus Christ. The framed pictures were about the only thing keeping the peeling paper on the wall.

"Welcome to my temple," she intoned in a church voice, then spread her arms and gathered both detectives into a warm embrace, as though they were long lost sons returning home from the Crusades. The broad cloth of her sleeves slipped around them like wings, and they felt smothered.

"You've come to me for salvation," she said. "I will help you fight the temptations of lust that prey upon young men in this city. The T.V. billboards and films, those icons composed by Satan himself. The whores who taunt your flesh."

"There's been some mistake," Santillo interrupted. "We thought that Matt Christian lived here—"

"My son," she said proudly. "As fine a Christian as there is," and she laughed at the pun. "Did he send you to witness my work? Come, let me show you the rest of the temple."

With a firm grip on their elbows she propelled them down the hall to the arched entrance of a living room, above which was a crucifix on a circle of bronzed thorns. Inside the room two old-timers were leaning elbows on knees and glaring at each other across a chess board. On a tattered sofa that was losing its stuffing a man was sleeping, a magazine V-ed over his face.

"Mr. Smith and Mr. Jones have come to my temple in search of peace," she whispered loudly to Santillo and Weston, then addressed the two chess players: "You've come to my temple in search of peace, haven't you gentlemen?"

They nodded without looking up from the chess pieces. They'd put in a lifetime agreeing with people in order to get a handout and they weren't about to stop now.

"They have turned their backs on sinful temptation," she incanted, and then remarked privately to the detectives: "The city is overrun with temptations.

Any night of the week you can look out the window and see the streets fill up with Satan's whores, their faces painted, wandering the streets in clothes that create the very lust they prey upon. Victimizing these poor men."

The poor victims playing chess did more nodding, but they didn't do any listening.

"Could we see Matt's room, Mrs. Christian?" Santillo asked.

"My son moved into a place of his own last month. But that won't stop him from fighting the good fight. He's a good Christian."

"Can you tell us where he lives now?"

"I'll get the address." She padded off down the hall, and one of the chess players looked up from the board and sent his bloodshot glance toward the two cops.

"If you're looking for peace," he said, "this isn't the place to find it. Not with her yakking all the time."

"We're looking for her son," Weston said. "You know him?"

A brief nod. "Spent all his time in the back yard breaking boards with his hands. Quieter than her, but just as weird. Treated her like a queen and everybody else around her like shit. Glad he's gone." He went back to contemplating his next chess move, and Weston decided to have a quick look around. He pushed open the door across the hall and found a dim room that looked like a temple: a couple of wooden chairs arranged around an altar piece that consisted of a statue of Christ on the cross. On each of the four walls hung a crucifix on a circle of bronzed thorns.

Mrs. Christian returned, bearing an address book and a Bible.

"'Be sure your sin will find you out,'" she quoted gravely, and went on reading passages for a time before Weston could get her around to giving up her son's address. She gave them a number in the East Village.

"He is my evangelist," she said, as they went out the front door. "He is my hands and my roots and he carries on the good work..."

In the car the two men looked at each other.

"Crazy as a loon," Weston said.

"Which gives me a bad feeling about her son."

The bad feeling was mutual.

Dawn Palmer was in the dressing room when the acne-skinned girl poked her head in and said, "Telephone, Dawn."

She took the call at the hall phone outside the dressing room. It was Mitch Roundtree.

"Are you free to meet Mr. Lancia's rep this afternoon?" he asked. "I showed him your pics but he's a tough cookie, and he won't okay a photo session until he's had a look at you in the flesh."

"Where should I meet him?" He gave her the address of an office building on Twenty-eighth Street.

"I've rented room 274," he told her. "Be there by seven. And, Dawn, look your A-one best. If he likes you, we'll start shooting tonight."

"Tonight? I've already put in a full day."

"It won't kill you," he said, and as he hung up she could hear the faint sound of his laughter.

She finished touching up her hair. It was 4:15, the dinner hour at the studio, and the place was empty and quiet, only a couple of photographers left in the darkroom. At 6:30 it would come to life again when the evening sessions began.

Dawn Palmer was about to leave the studio when she remembered that she was supposed to meet Santillo at a restaurant at seven o'clock tonight. She called his office.

"Santillo's not in," she was told. "Can I take a message?"

"Tell him I can't make our dinner date tonight. Something important's come up. An assignment that I just can't turn down."

"Will do."

She left the studio a few minutes later then walked with freedom and confidence because she felt safe: she knew that somewhere in the crowded streets a police detective was watching her...

The door of Matt Christian's apartment was securely bolted. Santillo opened the fire case at the end of the hall and came back with the fire axe. He swung it hard, laying the blade an inch deep in a horizontal gash above the knob. He hit the door a couple more times, then slammed it with his shoulder and the door swung open, leaving the knob and bolts hanging in the frame.

The two detectives walked into a small, dark living room with only a few spartan furnishings: a hardback desk chair, an end table, an unpadded arm chair. Each wall supported one picture of Christ and a couple of crucifixes. A crucifix lay in a circle of stained glass that was hanging in the window.

The adjoining room had heavy drapes across the sunlit window. In the center of the room, votive candles burned around a cloth-draped table on which stood the now-familiar circle with the crucifix on it. But now the crucifix bore no Christ figure, it was just a cross, like the cross hairs of a rifle sight ... there were pillows on the floor in front of the table, as though to cushion the knees of a worshipper.

The door of the next room was locked but this time only one swing of the heavy axe was needed to open it. Santillo and Weston entered the room, and then stopped dead in their tracks when they caught sight of the walls: every square inch of wallspace was covered with pornographic pictures clipped from magazines. And not just the walls, the ceiling and floor also were one vast collage of overlapping pictures of naked breasts and female genitals. And painted in heavy black ink on almost every woman's genitals were the cross hairs and circle. There was a red bulb in the overhead socket, and it spilled eerie light across the walls and floor, creating a phantasmagoric, hallucinatory scene, making the pictures swim like corpses in the red light. Both Santillo and Weston had the uncanny feeling that they were standing at the hot center of a sick mind.

A mother who was obsessed with the sinning temptations of prostitutes, a domineering woman who wanted her son to rid the world of them; the ever-present crucifixes on a circle of thorns, transforming over the years into the cross hairs of a telescopic sight. Even his own surname stamping him with his mother's obsession. Matt Christian's lunatic motivations seemed to whirl through the erotic collage like a mist. ... Some pieces of the puzzle falling into place, others remaining just out of grasp. But that did not interest Santillo and Weston, that was for psychiatrists to argue over in court. The two detectives just wanted to get to Christian before he used his rifle again.

Santillo put a call through to headquarters, talked to the dispatcher for men on police surveillance.

"Has Matt Christian checked in today?"

"Not yet. But he seldom does."

Santillo called the Jenkins Studio. Dawn Palmer was not in. The receptionist had not seen Christian.

"If he's not following her," Santillo told Weston, "she could be in danger."

"Let's shake this place down."

Their search of the apartment was quick and thorough. Under a loose floorboard in the closet they found a vinyl-lined compartment between the joists. It contained a case for a high-powered rifle. The rifle was missing.

"If he's got the gun with him now," Santillo pointed out, "that means he's going to use it."

"But where the hell is the bastard going to hit next?" Weston wanted to know.

They continued their search of the apartment. When Weston riffled the pages of a stack of magazines, a folded piece of paper fell out. Weston unfolded it. It was a map of New York City, and on it Christian had marked the sites of his three snipings. The three areas bore a circle with cross hairs, and written beside them was the date of the attack, and the body count, as in a parody of a war campaign map.

"He's marked a fourth area," Weston noticed.

The fourth circle and cross hairs encompassed the point where Broadway joined Seventh Avenue, just north of Times Square. From that vantage point a long rifle could draw a bead on pedestrian traffic for blocks up and down the busiest streets in the world.

The dead center of the circle was the Dunham Building, which occupied an entire city block, a small concrete island where Seventh Avenue angles into Broadway. It took Santillo and Weston fifteen minutes to reach it. When they arrived, there was a prowl car parked at the curb in front, but no sign of its passengers.

Inside the building Santillo and Weston went to the office of the building security chief.

"The other two cops just got here a minute ago," the security chief told them. "They're around somewhere...."

"How many men to you have on staff today?" Weston asked.

"Just me," he replied apologetically.

Santillo and Weston took his master keys, then left him guarding the front door while they started a search of the building. Santillo took the second floor and Weston the third. They moved from room to room, carefully checking each place that might offer Christian a sniper's nest....

Five minutes before Santillo and Weston arrived, the Dunham Building janitor dragged the last of the garbage bags out of the side entrance, and deposited it on the curb at the corner of Forty-eighth and Broadway, then returned inside, letting the door swing closed behind him.

Matt Christian stepped casually out of the passing crowd, and reached the door an instant before the latch was about to slide in. He waited a moment to be sure the janitor was well on his way, then pushed the door open and walked down a short flight of steps into the building's dark basement. The darkness throbbed with the mechanical beat of big boilers. Sweating pipes ran mazes overhead.

Christian took a concrete path that skirted big wire-mesh storage bins and ended at a stairway door. Before he got to the door, however, it opened and the janitor reentered the basement. Christian stopped in the shadows, put down his Adidas bag, and readied his hands to kill the janitor. But the man did not come toward Christian. He disappeared around a corner and reappeared a while later. He went on up the stairs, whistling softly to himself. Christian waited motionless a long time, and when it was obvious the janitor wasn't returning, he picked up the Adidas bag and continued toward the stairway door.

He was breathing a little easier when he got to the door, and had just put his hand on the knob, when a deep voice sounded in the darkness to the right:

"Hold it right there, turkey."

A big black uniformed cop held his gun level with Christian's stomach. Next to him stood another cop, this one with cuffs ready in his hands.

"Spread eagle against the wall, fella," the second cop advised. He was older, more seasoned and less hostile than the other.

"There must be some mistake," Christian objected.

"Yeah, and you made it, turkey."

"I'm a cop," Christian stated.

"We know who you are and what you are," the older cop said. He could not keep out of his voice the disgust an honest cop naturally feels for a cop who had gone bad. "Detective Weston put a request on the air for a squad car to get over here and wait for you."

"Weston..." Anger burned in Christian.

"That's right. Now make it easy on yourself, and spread 'em against the wall."

"Sure," Christian said, and now the anger was gone, replaced by the resolve to kill these two men, or die trying.

He turned and braced himself against the wall. He held the position for perhaps ten seconds, then he spun around, lifting and kicking his right foot as he turned. As he'd expected, the older cop was just crossing his partner's line of fire, and the foot caught the cop in the pelvis, knocking him straight back into his partner. As the two men stumbled off balance Christian kicked again and the toe of his shoe caught the cop's gun hand and the revolver went spinning off into a tangle of low-lying boiler pipes. The younger cop was first to regain his composure, and he warned his partner:

"Keep away from this guy, he's using karate."

"Try using karate on this bullet," the older cop challenged and started to pull his own gun out.

Christian made a spinning lunge at the younger cop to hold him back, then he ended his spin with two quick jabs of his fists at the older cop, the first hitting him in the side with bone-crushing force, the second stabbing into the man's neck with devastating power: the man's windpipe collapsed and his neck snapped sideways with a sharp cracking noise and the guy went down as though a building had fallen on him. He was still breathing, but Christian's first punch had paralyzed him and all he could do was lie there. Christian smashed the edge of his foot right across the cop's throat again, and the neck snapped back the other way, limp as a rag doll's, and the last glitter of life disappeared from the man's eyes.

The other cop had his billy club out and he knew how to use it: wielding it like a sword he thrust twice, then cut the air with a vicious swing for Christian's head. But years of training took over and almost without thinking Christian dodged and pivoted away from the lunging cop, flinging out a foot that hit the guy a glancing blow on the hip. The cop fell off balance and Christian went for him with another kick, but the cop was quick as well as strong and he smashed the club across Christian's thigh, got to his feet and came at Christian swinging the club.

The blow missed Christian and smashed into a boiler pipe, and steam started leaking into the already humid atmosphere of the basement. Christian clipped the cop's hand with a hard blow and the billy club fell, but the cop wasn't daunted: he came straight for Christian, arms pumping fists the size of cantaloupes. The cop was bigger and stronger than Christian, and obviously a seasoned fighter, but his punches were not aimed with the lethal accuracy of martial arts training. Any one of Christian's blows could have killed the guy if they had landed properly. And finally one of them did: he snapped the hard edge of his open hand across the bridge of the cop's nose, breaking the nose, and then with the heel of his palm he pushed the guy's nose straight up into the brain. The sharp point of broken cartiledge pierced the brain, and the man crumpled to the floor of the basement. Even though the cop was dead, Christian delivered an insurance blow with his foot, then carried both bodies into a corner of the basement and threw a tarp over them.

He had escaped capture, but wasn't out of the woods yet. Winning one fight didn't amount to a hill of beans. Santillo and Weston knew he was the sniper. His crusade against the prostitutes would end tonight. There was no escaping that fact. And that meant that he would die tonight, before he could finish his appointed task. The last savior had tried to cleanse the world with peace and He had been crucified for His trouble; now Christian had tried to cleanse it with violence and he would meet the same fate.

In a way it was a relief—no more running, no more hiding and lying. One last stand against the evil forces. He would die, but in doing so he would take many of them with him. His Adidas bag was heavy with ammunition—he always carried a couple of hundred extra loads to provide for just such a contingency. Yes, he would take many of them with him. He would certainly take Weston with him, if it was the last thing he ever did. . . .

Christian went back to the stairway and started climbing. At the third floor he opened the door a crack. He was right across the hall from the unoccupied office he had planned to use as his sniper's nest. The hall was empty. He started to cross to the door when he heard a sound and he pulled back. A moment later he saw Weston come around the corner at the end of the hall and start this way, checking rooms as he came.

Christian was sure that in Weston's search he would open this stairway door. And when he did, he would get the surprise of his life.

Christian put his Adidas bag down on the stairs, then unscrewed the wall light bulb, plunging the landing into darkness. He stood in the corner opposite the door, and assumed a karate attack stance, feet apart, hands balled into hard fists, arms cocked and ready. And he waited, relaxed, a small crescent of white teeth gleaming through a half-smile of anticipation.

As Weston approached the stairway door, a pallid young man with a scholar's stoop to his thin shoulders came out of a law office and headed for the same door. He reached it a second before Weston did, put his hand on the knob and started to push.

Weston grabbed his hand, pulled the young lawyer away from the door. Poised, thinking, Weston raised a hand to silence the young man, who was about to ask a question: Weston didn't want anybody making a sound, and besides that, he couldn't have explained what the problem was. He didn't know what had made him stop the young man from opening that door, but something had told him things were wrong. In the cop business, if you're any good at your work, you develop an instinct for survival, and if you're paying attention to your work you'll stop and listen to that instinct when it warns you. And right now warning sirens were going off in Weston's head, and he was trying to figure out why. After a moment he spotted the reason.

The doors of this office building were loose-fitting, especially this particular stairway door, and that meant that a person should be able to see light from the stairway seeping under the door. But there was no light under this one. Which meant that the light was out. Burnt out, or a trap?

He motioned the young lawyer to one side, drew his .38, and took a step back from the door, then he charged the door, slamming it open with his foot and going out onto the landing at an angle, his body low, his gun ready. All that met him out there was darkness.

"Are you some sort of a madman?" the young man asked from the hallway. He was staring at Weston with a kind of amused amazement, as though wondering if the cop were certifiable.

But as Weston was getting to his feet he heard the soft tread of footsteps somewhere above him, and he looked up through the iron slats of the stairs and saw a shadow moving upward, a shadow carrying a bag. He'd been out here, all right, and something had spooked him and he'd moved on: the hunter is not the only one with instincts, Weston thought, the quarry has them, too.

Weston started up the steps and as soon as he did, Christian started running, too. Eight tall stories to the roof. A tough climb to make on the dead run, even for a man in the best of physical condition, which Weston was, and he started tiring two-thirds of the way up, his breath hot and heavy in his aching lungs, his legs two lead bars that required enormous effort to lift. But he didn't let up, and he was gaining on Christian, was only a half a flight behind when he heard a woman's scream from above and suddenly saw the woman herself as she came flying down the stairs at him, her arms windmilling for balance. She collided with Weston and the two of them staggered down a few steps and crashed onto the lower landing. It took Weston a few seconds to extricate himself from her long legs and arms and tangle of skirt, and by that time he'd lost a lot of ground to Christian.

Christian went out onto the roof. When Weston got there Christian had made it across to the base of a huge elevated water tank. Christian crouched behind one of the massive support legs of the tank. Night was still hours away, but the sun was low behind the tall buildings in the west, and the sky was gradually losing its fight against darkness. It was fairly dark on the roof. Window and marquee lights were blazing in the streets below, erecting faint milky walls beyond the parapet.

Weston ran out after Christian. He couldn't give the guy time enough to put together his rifle: once he did that, it was game over, not only for Weston, but probably for dozens of innocent people in the streets: Christian knew he was cornered and he was the kind of obsessed man who—knowing he would die—would end his life with one long, bloody last stand.

Christian broke cover immediately and ran a weaving trail to the far end of the roof, where an enormous billboard jutted straight up into the sky. The billboard was as broad as the whole building, and almost as tall. On the street side the picture was of a long-legged woman in a black evening dress; she was draped over the hood of a luxury car along with a couple of jungle cats. On this side of the picture a lattice-work of metal beams and bars, struts and supports, scaled the billboard to a narrow platform at the top.

Christian started climbing into the supports. Weston fired his .38. A bullet clanged off the strut under Christian's foot, but it did not slow him up, and in another second he had dissolved into the shadows of the billboard, shielded by the interweaving supports. Weston had no choice but to climb up after him.

Ten feet off the ground Weston saw Christian straddling a horizontal support and taking the two pieces of his rifle out of the Adidas bag. He hung the stock around his neck by its strap, tucked the barrel and the telescopic sights into his belt, and then he started filling his pockets with packets of ammunition. He must have had a hundred rounds of ammo, and Weston realized that each time Christian went out to kill he carried with him the idea that this particular sniping might be his final stand, maybe at the back of his mind even carried the *hope* that it would be the final time. Maybe this final stand was what all the snipings were about.

Weston braced himself against the supports and freed his gun from the hip holster. He took aim, and as he was squeezing off a shot, Christian scuttled sideways across a strut and the slug penetrated nothing but shadows. The next thing Weston knew, he was being slapped in the face by the empty Adidas bag and he slipped from his perch. In order to save himself from falling, he had to let go of his gun. He heard the .38 clang off the metalwork and then hit the roof with a spongy sound. He didn't know exactly where it had landed, but it probably would not be hard to find. The problem was that he didn't have time to retrieve it and still get to Christian before he'd got that rifle put together, and a .38 was no match for a high-powered rifle: a .38 slug hit you in the leg and you could hobble or crawl to safety, but when a rifle slug like Christian's hit your leg, you never walked again, and even crawling is a difficult task without your leg.

Weston pulled himself upward, hand over hand, propping himself with elbows and hips, like an acrobat heading for the trapeze platform. He was sweating profusely and at one point near the top he almost fell when a smooth metal support slipped out from under his sweat-slicked hand.

Christian hoisted himself onto the narrow ledge at the top of the billboard. Weston reached the ledge a few seconds later, lifted his head above the edge, and then immediately ducked back as Christian's foot cut viciously through the air where his head had come up. Weston weaved between the supports to a point a few feet to the left, and then pulled himself up. Christian was five yards away, kneeling on the platform and starting to fasten the rifle barrel to its stock. When he saw Weston he noticed for the first time that Weston had no gun, and a smile came to his boyish face.

"Lose your gun, tough guy?" he asked playfully, then went on grimly: "Without your armament, you're nothing to me, Weston, nothing. I remember a while back I asked you what you'd do if I came at you with these"—he held up his hands like prized weapons—"and you said you'd put a bullet into my skull. How are you going to get it in there now, huh?"

He laid the dismantled gun to one side, laying the oilskin over it as though putting it to bed for the night, then he calmly got to his feet and walked toward Weston.

"You like heights, Weston?" Christian sneered.

Weston didn't mind heights when the four walls and solid floor of a building supported him, but up here there was nothing for support but a three-foot-wide ledge, and the warm night air. On one side of the billboard was a sixty-foot fall to the building roof, on the other a two-hundred-foot fall to pavement. And Christian was bent on making Weston take one of those two falls. As Christian came nearer, Weston backed up, remembering his last encounter with the agile, lethal kicks of those feet.

"You can only go so far before you're walking on air," Christian told him. "Not as tough as you thought you were, huh, my friend? You know how fragile your throat is? Let me show you." Christian turned to the upper edge of the billboard which rose about three feet above the walkway. He seemed to study it a moment, then with blurring speed he flung the calloused edge of his hand down on the wood, and it snapped. "Your throat's not that tough."

Weston's throat went prickly as the splintered wood lying under Christian's hand.

"I don't think I'll kill you right away," Christian mused, as Weston kept on backing away. "I think what I'll do," he went on with sadistic glee, "is break your neck. That will paralyze you, even though you won't feel much pain. I won't heave you overboard right away, though. What I'll do is prop you up so you can watch me shoot for a while, watch all the people die that you were stupid enough to think you could save." He kept on advancing on Weston.

Karate—or any other of the oriental martial arts, for that matter—is not some mysterious weapon that you can pull out whenever you need it. Like everything else in life, Weston knew, if it was to be used for maximum effect it required unflagging concentration. If the necessary concentration was lacking your opponent gained an advantage. If a man is to fight well, his mind and body must work in harmony. So Weston decided to try to throw a little disharmony Christian's way:

"Santillo and I talked to your mother today," he said, and he knew he had chosen the right subject when he saw Christian's step falter and his eyes narrow with anger. "She's quite a woman."

"You leave my mother alone!"

"She sends her love."

"You bastard! I know what you really think of her, you think she's crazy. But she's not. She's the only sane person in this insane world, she's a saint." He surged at Weston quickly, expecting Weston to continue to retreat, but Weston came right at Christian and took him by surprise. Weston received a solid chopping blow on the side that made him gasp in pain, but he retaliated by plunging his fist up to the wrist in Christian's stomach, and the two men went into a clinch. Weston did his best to hang on to Christian because he knew that part of karate's power came from the momentum gained by uninhibited movement—it's for open spaces, not confined ones.

They traded a couple of blows, then Christian jammed an elbow into Weston's ribs, and broke free. He swung an open palm like an axe at Weston's neck. Weston blocked the swing with a forearm, hit Christian two quick blows to the midsection. Christian staggered back and his legs caught the billboard edge and he nearly went over the side, but he righted himself and kicked out at Weston. His foot hammered Weston's thigh with bruising force, driving the detective back a pace, but not keeping him from charging into the guy, fists flying. Weston rained punches at Christian, clipped him on the chin, the shoulder, the arm and chest, the chin again. In return, Weston had to stand up against Christian's carefully directed punches, and he felt them taking their toll, but he didn't give an inch, kept pressing in and hammering away at Christian's midsection. At last it looked like Christian was tiring, and he swayed a bit, then seemed to collapse into Weston's arms. But he wasn't tiring that much, it was an act so that he could slip in under Weston's punches. And it worked.

Christian gripped the loose collar of Weston's coat and tried to lever him over the billboard frame. They both crashed into the frame, Christian on top, and he jammed the palm of his left hand under Weston's chin and started pushing, and Weston's head was forced over the edge of the billboard, further and further out as Christian increased the pressure. Weston felt his shoulders slipping out over the edge. Then Christian got his other hand free and brought it up and then sharply down in a karate chop aimed at Weston's throat. Weston twisted sideways and the chop hit him a glancing blow that instantly numbed the side of his neck. He rolled out from under another karate chop, then he made as if to scramble sideways away from Christian, but quickly pivoted and dived for the guy's knees. He brought Christian down on the ledge. Christian aimed a kick at Weston's face, missed, but hit Weston in the chest and knocked the breath out of him. Separated, both men got to their feet, and stood a moment, weary arms sagging, like a couple of punch-drunk fighters.

There were shouts from the rooftop below them as Santillo led a couple of cops across to the base of the billboard. It was over for Christian and he seemed to realize it. Even if he could get rid of Weston, the others would be on him before he could get the rifle assembled. He looked fondly at the two pieces of the rifle, as if silently saying goodbye to a friend, then started closing the distance between himself and Weston. A wild light burned in his crazed eyes, lines of anger were entrenched in his face. He didn't care about defeating Weston now, but he wasn't going to settle for anything less than taking Weston over the edge with him.

A few steps from Weston he paused and changed his stance, as though preparing himself for a kick.

"This is it, Weston. The end of the road. I die, but you die with me." Then, in a mild voice he added: "When I killed Jessica Newman and you caught up with me on that roof, I beat you with my feet. I'll beat you with my feet tonight, too. . . ."

Weston's eyes dipped to watch his feet, and that was when Christian made his move. But not with his feet. Christian launched his whole body at the detective, swinging his arm in a wide arc meant to catch Weston in the side and carry both of the men over the side.

Sometimes you have to risk it all, including your life, on a single decision, and sometimes the situation demands that you act now, *now*, giving you no chance for analysis or second thoughts. For Weston that time had come, and when it did he played a hunch: he decided to ignore Christian's feet. He let his eyes dip to Christian's feet, but then immediately dropped to one knee. As Christian's arm swung over Weston's ducked head, Weston punched him hard in the side, and Christian was pushed over the edge. He tried to reach out and grab one of the spotlight supports on the billboard, but he was past them before he realized he'd been outsmarted. His body moved in a slowly rolling fall through twilight air to the sidewalk.

Weston climbed down the support structure to the roof. He was met by half a dozen uniformed cops and Santillo who quietly gave him his dropped .38. A couple of cops clapped him on the back as though he'd just scored the winning points in the championship game, but Weston grimly shrugged off the praise. He'd been lucky to survive, and he knew it. He'd made a guess up there that Christian was going to use his hands and not his feet. And he'd guessed right ... this time.

Santillo and Weston left the uniforms to clean up, while they went back down to their car. Weston sat and massaged his bruised muscles while Santillo put through radio calls to try to locate Dawn Palmer.

"No luck, Wes," he said, after a while. "She might be at the Jenkins Studio, but the line is busy."

"Let's get over and have a look."

"You feel up to it?"

But the question was lost in the roar of the motor as Weston pulled the Plymouth into traffic and started heading uptown.

8

The Jenkins Studio was empty except for the acned girl reading the latest edition of *Vogue* at the reception desk.

"If you're here for the evening sessions, they don't start for another half hour," she announced to Santillo and Weston as soon as they were in the door.

"N.Y.P.D.," Santillo returned. "Is Dawn Palmer here?"

"No. She left over an hour ago."

"Where to?"

The girl shrugged. "Shopping she said. Had to look her best to meet somebody's rep."

"Meet who, where?"

But the girl didn't know. "She came back in a second later and made a telephone call," the girl remembered. "To police headquarters. She had to break a dinner date in order to take an important assignment."

"What assignment? Did she say where?"

The girl shrugged.

Santillo telephoned Dawn Palmer's agent, who

said she knew nothing about a meeting with anyone today.

"I don't like it, Wes," Santillo said as he hung up. "Mysterious meeting. It fits the pattern."

"Where did she go to do the shopping?" Weston asked the receptionist.

"She didn't say," the girl replied. "But a lot of the models here get their stuff at L'Etranger. The owner there gives them a discount.

Another phone call, this one answered by a Brooklyn-accented French accent that told Santillo that Dawn Palmer had just left. He didn't know where to, he didn't see anyone following her.

After the call the two detectives just looked at each other. Helpless. They knew that somewhere in the city, Dawn Palmer was on her way to a meeting with a killer. And there was nothing they could do to prevent it. They were both picturing in their minds' eye the photograph of Dawn Palmer that had depicted the mutilation she was in for, and it made their flesh crawl. They had to curb the impulse to run down to L'Etranger and try to pick up her trail from there—doing that would make them feel like they were doing something useful, but it would not be productive and would take up a lot of valuable time, and at the moment time was the one thing they did not have much of. They took the receptionist back over her story of Dawn's departure.

"Did Dawn talk to anybody before she left, maybe tell them where she went?"

"She didn't tell me, and there's no one else around, won't be for another ten minutes or so, when the dinner break is over."

Another dead end.

"Wait a sec!" the girl exclaimed. "Alison was back there somewhere, maybe Dawn told her."

"Who's Alison?"

"One of the light technicians. She was checking the lights for the next session. At least that's what she was supposed to be doing. More likely she was laying one of the photographers. She'll do anything to break into the business."

When Santillo and Weston found Alison she was adjusting the positions of the floodlights that stood in an arc around the studio's main floor. A short balding guy with a Leica resting on his paunch was telling her how to arrange the lights.

"Are you Alison?" Santillo asked. She said she was. "Were you in the studio when Dawn Palmer took a call today?"

She was, and judging by the blush that fired her cheeks, she had been busy doing precisely what the receptionist had guessed. But all she gave the two detectives was another dead end:

"Dawn didn't tell me where she was going."

Then Santillo startled everybody: "Hold it!" he said.

The others looked at him: he had raised his nose a bit and was sniffing the air, and Alison and the photographer started to back away from him as though from a madman.

"What's that smell, that soapy smell?" Santillo asked.

It was coming from a hand towel that had been left on a wooden stool. Its heavy fibers were laden with the same sweet smell that Santillo had noticed in Melissa's hotel room, and then again faintly in the hall outside his own apartment. The towel bore a monogrammed M.R. in one corner.

"Who is M.R.?"

"That's Mitch Roundtree's hand towel," the photographer told him. "He uses that heavily scented soap to cover the chemical smells of the photographic baths."

"Anybody else here use this particular brand of soap?"

"We all use something strongly-scented, but nothing quite like that. He's kind of a fanatic on the subject."

"Any idea where Roundtree is right now?"

Alison shook her head, and the photographer said, "I should know. He and I live in the same neighborhood and I saw him leaving his building when I left mine a couple of hours ago. He was getting into a cab and he told the driver...." His voice drifted into silence as his mind drifted into the past. There was no clock ticking away in the silent studio, but against one wall was a big electric clock with a white dial and pitch black hands, and the two detectives could both see the second hand sweeping across the white, pushing a slowly accumulating mass of seconds into the past, an ominous black hand that could almost be seen pushing Dawn Palmer closer to her meeting with a killer. Yet neither cop interrupted the silence, for fear of fracturing the man's fragile remembering.

"Twenty-eighth and Park Avenue," the photographer said at last. "Yeah, Twenty-eighth and Park. I'm pretty sure that's what Mitch told the cabbie."

Santillo and Weston were on their way out the door.

* * *

Dawn Palmer arrived outside the Grover Building a full twenty-five minutes early. This area was full of business offices, and there were not a lot of boutiques in which it would be easy for a woman to kill time, so rather than wait around outside she decided to go on up to the appointed room. It did no harm to be early, especially with someone as big in the business as Lancia was. As she passed through the revolving doors of the Grover Building she glanced up and caught sight of Santillo across the street. It startled her: this marked the first time she had seen any one of the cops when they had been tailing her. She pushed on through and crossed the entrance lobby to the elevator. On the way up to the second floor it occurred to her that this was not Santillo's shift to be watching her, it was Matt Christian's. What then was Santillo doing in this area? She thought back to his intense face. His glance had been moving though the crowds. Not the way a man would glance if he were trying to appear casual; it was more like a man searching the streets for someone... for her perhaps? Dangerous possibilities suddenly blossomed in her mind like dank flowers.

The doors opened on the second floor, and she hesitated. She was early for the appointment and could easily afford to waste a few minutes by going back down and talking to Santillo. It would ease her mind. She took the elevator back down to the lobby.

When the doors opened Mitch Roundtree was standing in front of her.

"You're a bit early," he said.

"I know. I was just on my way out to—make a call."

"You can make it from the room," he said. "Sorry I wasn't there to meet you." He moved into the elevator, blocking her exit without seeming to. He did it adroitly, but there was something in the taut way he held his body, the way he leaned slightly forward as if in anticipation, that struck a disharmonious chord in Dawn, and the dank flowers in her mind spread like weeds.

The doors opened on the second floor and he offered his arm like a gentleman and ushered her down the hall to room 274. But she balked at going inside without first knowing what Santillo was doing in this neighborhood.

"I think maybe I should make the call downstairs," she said, and had turned to leave, when Mitch Roundtree grabbed her by the arm and dragged her into the room. He closed and locked the door, then gave her a hard shove. She tripped and fell in a heap at the foot of an armchair, her skirt riding up around her thighs. He stared a moment at the fading sunlight salting the fine hairs of her tanned thighs, then knelt in front of her and pressed a flat palm against her chest when she tried to get up.

"You were a tough one to catch," he told her. "And in spite of all my work, you almost got away. But now you're in the net, you are mine." His eyes flashed. "And now, while you are taking off your clothes, I'll explain the ground rules to you."

"You're insane."

He slapped her with the back of his hand and his signet ring opened a cut along her chin.

"You've already violated rule number one," he claimed. "Do *everything* I say, *when* I say it, and don't give me any backtalk. Now...take off your clothes."

The Cadillac pulled to the curb, and Farah got out of the front seat, took a quick look up and down the street for any sign of Ramad, found none, and then opened the door for the hakim. Farah led the way across to the elevators and then up to the appointed room.

Mitch Roundtree opened the door before they had even had time to knock.

"She's in the next room," he told them, and led them into the adjoining room, where Dawn Palmer was sitting on the couch, tears filling her wide blue eyes. Her dress was ripped at the shoulder, her stockings torn. A bruise was blooming blue on her cheekbone.

The hakim walked over to her, studied her with his head to one side, as though inspecting a particularly dilectable cut of meat. He walked around her once, then reached over and ran his fingers lightly through her hair. When she cringed away, he slapped her, and she was still. He reached into her dress and felt her breast, hefting it like a melon.

"She'll do," he said to Roundtree, then to her: "Are you frightened, my dear girl? A little, perhaps?"

"You make me sick," she asserted. "But you don't frighten me."

"Ah, a feisty one," he said with glee. "Excellent. I like a little resistance. But you are wrong not to be frightened. I've brought something that might frighten you a bit," he added, and patted his groin. "But it will surely delight you as well."

He took off his robes while Farah and Roundtree strapped her to the couch.

Faces. Male, female, young, old. Thousands of different faces, no two even remotely alike once you gave them a close look. It staggered the imagination that there could be such variety in the human face. It staggered Santillo's imagination, anyway, because he seemed to be having to look at each and every possible arrangement of facial features, except the pair he wanted to see, Dawn Palmer's or Mitch Roundtree's.

He had covered Park Avenue from Twenty-seventh to Twenty-ninth, and now he started doing the cross streets. Suddenly, the faces weren't different at all, but all seemed the same, had blurred together to form a single vague, featureless face.

Looking for a needle in a haystack. That's what both cops felt they were doing, but they kept on moving, watching, kept repeating Dawn's description to people on the street, and kept getting the same negative response.

"What we need is a picture of her," said Weston.

That was when Santillo spotted Dawn's picture on the cover of a magazine in a kiosk on Twenty-eighth Street. He and Weston went over and asked for two copies of *Fashion Today*, and got a funny look from the newsie.

"I'd think a couple of guys like you would be more interested in *Playboy*," joked the newsie, a thin guy with a nose like a beak. "Good looking woman," the newsie added, indicating the cover photo of Dawn. "The picture does her justice."

The two detectives lost all thoughts about leaving the kiosk.

"How can you be sure?" Santillo asked.

"I just saw her walk by. Not half an hour ago."

"Are you sure?"

"Sure, I'm sure. When you see a woman like that, you really give her a look."

"You see which way she went?"

The newsie pointed to the canopied entrance of an office building halfway down the block. When Santillo and Weston walked into the lobby, a night janitor—a grizzled old man of uncertain race—was polishing the brass around the elevators. He hadn't seen Dawn Palmer enter the place and didn't recognize Mitch Roundtree's description.

Santillo and Weston went over to have a look at the office directory board on one wall. There were at least two dozen unlabeled rooms and offices.

"Some of those are empty apartments and offices," the janitor said as he scanned the board. "But some of the unlabeled ones are occupied, it's just that the occupants don't like their names up. Let's see.... Four-twelve is empty. Seven-eighteen is empty. Two-seventy-four is, too. No, I take that back. That was rented just this week—"

"Just this week?" Santillo said.

"By a photographer as I recall. I never saw the guy myself..."

The two detectives borrowed the janitor's key to 274, then went up in the elevator. They walked quickly but quietly to the room in question. Santillo unlocked the door then, together, the two cops opened the door and walked in with their guns drawn. The room was empty, and dark except for a bar of light under the door on the right. Santillo and Weston pushed open the door, and went into the room. Dawn Palmer lay spread-eagle on the couch, arms and legs tied, her own panties stuffed in her mouth. Abdul Abidi was kneeling over her and roughly fondling her body. He was singing to himself in Arabic. Mitch Roundtree and the bodyguard Farah were sitting in the corner, like a couple of spectators at a movie house.

No one of them moved, except Dawn Palmer who was squirming to get out from under Abdul Abidi's touch.

"Everybody on your feet," Weston ordered.

The three men obeyed.

"Now, all of you, put your hands behind your backs, turn around and touch the wall with your nose."

They just stared at Weston, not knowing whether or not he was serious.

"You're joking," Farah said.

"Do I sound like I'm joking?" Weston asked with deadly calm, and they wasted no time doing as he had ordered.

While Santillo untied Dawn Palmer, Weston frisked the other three. He lifted an automatic off Farah, and a long-bladed butcher's knife off Mitch Roundtree.

About this time Abdul Abidi found his voice. "Do—do you realize who I am?" the hakim demanded. "I am the most revered hakim Abdul Abidi. I am a guest in your country."

"You just wore out your welcome, pal," Weston told him. "Now put your pants on."

Weston laid the gun and knife aside, and waited for the hakim to get into his pants. After a moment he heard a voice behind him say:

"Don't move. Don't even turn around, just drop the guns without any fuss."

It was a voice he recognized: Yusef Ramad. Weston put his gun down on the carpeted floor next to his feet and Ramad laughed softly. "Kick it away from you, my friend," he said to Weston. "You forget that at the museum I saw what you can do with guns."

Weston gave the gun a little nudge and turned around. There were six of them, all cut from the same mold, squat muscular bodies, dark broad faces, narrow dark eyes like slits in a fortress wall. All of them carried silenced automatics, except for one guy who carried a single-barrel, pump-action shotgun.

Ramad kept his automatic trained on Santillo and Weston while his pals grabbed the hakim and dragged him out of the room.

"Ramad," the hakim said with a whine threading his thin voice, "don't take me back there."

"Your countrymen want you."

"Please ... if it's money you want, all I have is yours—"

"I don't want your money."

"What then? Power? Every man has his price."

"Your corpse is my asking price."

Then the hakim lapsed into an Arabic dialect, his voice full of apology and pleading as he was half-carried through the next room and out into the hall.

Ramad waited until his men were well away from the room, then moved his gun to Farah, and shot him in the heart. A second shot followed, hitting the dead man in the forehead, and exploding out the back of his skull.

Ramad offered no farewell speeches, no regrets or explanations; killing Farah disturbed him about as much as turning out a light. The gun bucked twice again and Mitch Roundtree, who had opened his mouth to speak, dropped where he stood, blood swelling across his white shirtfront. The gun's hollow eye moved to stare at Weston.

Then three things happened at once. Weston made a dive for his gun, Dawn Palmer screamed, and Santillo flung the hakim's discarded robes at Ramad. The robes parachuted open in front of him, blocking his view and throwing off his shot so that the bullet hit the wall above the diving Weston. But Ramad recovered quick as a cat and, before either Santillo or Weston could get to their guns, Ramad had grabbed Dawn Palmer and pulled her out of the room with him.

Santillo and Weston picked up their guns and were at the door in time to see Ramad going into the hallway, pulling Dawn along after him as a shield. Ramad's friends had already cleared off the second floor. Ramad took the stairs near the elevator, and Santillo and Weston went down right behind him, looking for but unable to find an opening to shoot. In the lobby Ramad waited by the entrance until his friends had got the hakim into a Ford van parked in front of the building. Then, still holding Dawn Palmer as a shield, he let off a couple of shots to discourage Santillo and Weston and ran for the van.

The van leaped into the north-bound traffic as

Weston waved a cab to the curb, then pulled the driver out from under the wheel.

"Hey, what's the idea?"

"Police," was all Weston said, and the cabbie shrugged as though stealing automobiles were a new police function.

"If you have an accident," he called after them, "be sure to total it. I could use a new cab."

They were about a block behind the escaping van. Traffic was thick, slowing up both vehicles and making it difficult to keep the van in sight. While Weston negotiated the traffic, Santillo got on the radio. The cab dispatcher patched him through to police headquarters.

"Santillo and Weston driving a cab north on Park Avenue in pursuit of a blue and gray 1976 Ford van." He explained the situation and the information was relayed to police cars in the vicinity.

The van weaved in and out of traffic, clipping cars and sending them veering to avoid collisions. A big Mercury had to slam on the brakes to dodge the van, and spun out of control, coming to a stop sideways across the lane, blocking the cab's path. Weston yanked the steering wheel left and the speeding cab —tires squealing and spewing smoke—slid sideways into the lane of oncoming traffic. A *New York Times* delivery truck filling the lane tried to turn away, but Weston was moving too fast, and the truck sideswiped the cab. Weston's window shattered and his door gave a metallic whine as it scraped past the truck. Weston wrenched the wheel, and the cab jumped into its own lane again, ahead of the stalled Mercury.

The van widened its lead. It sneaked through the

red light at Forty-ninth, causing a minor accident that left the intersection irreparably jammed in its wake. Again Weston swung into the oncoming traffic and, horn blaring, maneuvered between cars and into the intersection. But the intersection was impassable. He kicked into reverse, backed out of the intersection, turned in between two parked cars, and swung up onto the sidewalk. Pedestrians scattered like frightened pigeons and ran to doorways for safety. Half a block along, Weston turned off the sidewalk and cut diagonally across two lanes of traffic going the wrong way. The cab was hit three times, like unfriendly nudges directed at a guy rudely cutting into line, but none of them was serious enough to stop the cab.

The van had gained another block and was closing in on the intersection at Fifty-third when a patrol car appeared from the right, cut into the middle of Park Avenue and blocked the street. The van swerved, but not far or fast enough, and smashed the patrol car's side and the two vehicles careened, the van doing a slow 180 degree turn, like a compass needle at the Pole. When it came to a stop, the van's driver got the stalled engine going again, put it in reverse, backed up to get its grill free of the prowl car. The van hit a guy standing in the crosswalk. The surprised pedestrian went down under the right rear wheel, and the van bumped over him and then started dragging him away.

Weston came into the intersection with the brakes on. Santillo took aim at the driver of the van. Two slugs from Santillo's .38 starred the driver's window and the driver slumped forward and the surging van slowed—then surged again as the guy next to the dead driver reached across for the wheel and stomped on the gas.

It is difficult to handle any vehicle from the passenger seat, especially with a dead man slumped across the wheel, but the guy did a good job of it for three blocks, weaving with considerable accuracy between veering cars. He turned east on Fifty-ninth, sending two cars onto the curb to get away from him. But then the body of the dead driver sagged heavier across the steering wheel, and the guy started getting erratic. He clipped a couple of cars, and then overcompensated to avoid a truck, and went up over the curb, plowed right through a magazine kiosk, and then up four steps of a building on the corner of Lexington Avenue. The van crashed to a halt with its front end wedged in the building's front doors.

Santillo and Weston pulled up just a few seconds later, but in New York City, a few seconds is all the time that is needed to get half the population accumulated around an accident scene. People were standing three deep on the sidewalk when the back doors of the wrecked van popped open and Ramad and the others got out.

"Get back everybody!" Weston shouted. "These men are dangerous."

As if to prove the contention, one of Ramad's men raised his shotgun and fired. Three people in the crowd near the two cops were hit by buckshot, and then the rest of the people froze where they were. A couple of the gunmen grabbed bystanders and used them as shields. Fear cleared a path through the crowd for the Arab gunmen as they dragged their hostages away from the van.

A couple of prowl cars rounded the corner onto

Lexington. Instead of heading for the street, Ramad went to a subway entrance and down the steps. They backed down, holding their hostages in the line of fire, and disappeared around a corner below.

Santillo turned to a uniformed cop who had just arrived at the scene: "Get on the radio to headquarters and have them alert I.R.T. central dispatching to keep subway trains out of this station. Then seal off this entrance and all the others to this stop."

"Right."

Santillo and Weston went down the steps of the Fifty-ninth Street station. There were no people in sight below ground. They rounded a corner. Up ahead was the token booth, and across from the booth turnstyles stood across the mouth of a short tunnel that led to the subway train platforms. The booth operator was slumped over the counter, a bullet hole in the back of his head. The two detectives jumped the turnstyles and headed for the mouth of the tunnel.

They had taken only a few steps when one of the Arabs stepped out from behind a pillar, leveled his shotgun at them and fired in one swift motion. The silence of the underground station exploded. But even as he was shooting, Santillo and Weston were diving for the ground, one to each side, and rolling hard to get away from the blast of buckshot. The buckshot exploded into a turnstyle, rupturing it, and tokens started spilling out and rolling across the floor.

The Arab fired again at Weston, but Weston kept on rolling and managed to get behind one of the concrete pillars. The shotgun blast took a chunk out of the concrete and sent chips flying. As soon as Santillo saw the shotgun move after his partner, Santillo came to a stop on the damp tile floor and took aim at the Arab. His first shot hit the guy in the hip and the Arab seemed to fold in half sideways. But he didn't go down. He sagged over and—letting the wall hold him up—tried to draw a bead on Santillo. Santillo didn't give him time; he fed him another slug, this one in the side of the head. The Arab's skull gushed red, and he fell to the floor and was still.

"You okay?" Santillo asked his partner.

"Yeah," replied Weston, "but let's watch where the hell we're walking from now on."

Santillo and Weston cautiously entered the tunnel. As they came out the other end, they quickly moved behind a couple of posts that were situated nearby. From there they could see the station platform. Dozens of people who had been waiting for the next train were now lined up along the platform, hands over their heads, backs to the tracks. They formed a human wall, behind which stood Ramad and his four men with the hakim and Dawn Palmer. Even behind the wall of people the Arab gunmen took no chances, and were constantly pacing back and forth so as not to present a stationary target for a moment.

"If you try to interfer with us in any way," Ramad shouted to the detectives, "these people will be shot. And the first to die will be your precious fashion model."

He said something else, but it was drowned out by a swelling grumble from the tunnel as a train approached the station, ricketing on the tracks, wheels squealing on a turn. With a bit of luck, Santillo hoped, the I.R.T. dispatcher would manage to warn the train to stop short of the station, and leave the gunmen stranded where they were. But luck was all with the gunmen. The train entered the station, slowing.

The driver of the train wasn't paying much attention to the passengers on the platform—after four hours at the controls you tended to look without really seeing—and it wasn't until the train was well into the station that it occurred to him that the passengers were lined up oddly on the platform. Then he saw the Arabs and the guns in their hands, and decided the best thing to do was to keep on going right through the station. But he reversed that decision in an instant when Ramad pointed his automatic directly at him, and shouted for him to stop.

Santillo and Weston watched helplessly as the gunmen climbed into the lead subway car. None of the doors of the other cars had been opened. People inside those cars—not yet realizing what was happening—were calmly waiting for the doors to open so that they could get off. Then the subway train again lurched into motion and the passengers had to clutch at straps to keep their balance.

Santillo and Weston burst through the people remaining on the platform, and ran down the edge of the platform along side the subway train. The train gaining speed out of the station started to leave the cops behind. But when a space between two cars came along side him, Santillo picked up his pace to match the train's, reached out and grabbed the window frame, then jumped into the opening between cars. There was room to stand here—this was a favorite hideout of kids who would reach out and snatch purses from women on the platform as the train pulled out of the station—but it didn't offer much footspace to jump onto, just a couple of bumper-like projections less than eight inches wide. One of Santillo's feet landed firmly, but the other slipped on the smooth metal surface, and Santillo had to hang onto the window frame for all he was worth while he sought footing. Out of the corner of his eye he could see the entrance of the tunnel flying at him. His foot found firmer ground and he pulled himself between cars and then the tunnel wall swept up and by him, slapping at his coattails. He broke a window with his pistol butt, knocked out the glass and climbed into the car. The passengers were standing around staring open-mouthed at his entrance.

"Police," Santillo shouted above the clattering rumble of the speeding train. "Everybody get down on the floor. Move it!"

Weston had got on the train via the conductor's door in the last car. He did his best to calm people there, then moved up to the next car, where he found Santillo. They decided to move these passengers into the last car to keep them as far away from the gunmen as possible, an idea that appealed to the passengers, who immediately obeyed.

There were six cars in the train, and Santillo and Weston had managed to clear the last three before they met up with one of the gunmen. The Arab forced a group of passengers to sit in a tight-knit bunch at the far end of the car, and he was entrenched behind them, like a sniper in a bunker of living bodies. He sprayed the back of the car with bullets when Santillo and Weston appeared and the two cops had to hold down a position between cars and try to figure out their next move.

The subway train hurtled into the station at Fiftieth. The platform was crowded with passengers who were all lined up at the platform edge ready to get on the train. The train flew right through the station, and hurtled into the dark tunnel again, building speed.

The train had green lights all the way to Grand Central, and rattled along at high speed until just after it had cleared the platform at that station, and then without warning it started braking. Everybody on the train was thrown to the floor as the train came to a juddering stop in an empty stretch of track just beyond the station. The train sat there for a minute or two. Santillo and Weston went to the windows and kept an eye out for Ramad and the others, but no one left the train.

Then Santillo heard the train start to move again, but he did not feel the jolt of movement, and he looked up to see the lead car—uncoupled from the rest of the train—moving off down the tracks. Ramad had had no intention of getting off the train, he had simply stopped so that he could uncouple the lead car. Santillo and Weston took turns cursing themselves for not realizing sooner what Ramad had been up to. But there was nothing they could do about it now. There wouldn't have been anything they could do in any case, not without starting something that could too easily lead to a massacre of the passengers.

The lead car disappeared in the darkness ahead, then Santillo and Weston oversaw the debarkation of the passengers and led them back down the track to the station platform, where a handful of cops and subway security officers helped herd them to safety.

"You guys Santillo and Weston?" one of them

asked the detectives. "You're wanted upstairs, radio call from Lt. Hunt."

Santillo took the call, and told Lt. Hunt what had happened.

"He's still got the hostages?"

"Yes, sir. Besides the hakim and Dawn Palmer he's got a whole carload of passengers. I'd guess close to fifty people."

"Fifty! Jesus H. Christ!" It sounded as though Lt. Hunt were about to go on in that vein, when he interrupted himself with, "Hold on, I've got to take a call." He was back five minutes later. "That was I.R.T. Central. Ramad has been in touch with them already. He gave the guy a list of demands as long as a Mormon's clothesline. He's stopped the train between Forty-second and Thirty-third Street stations, and he's waiting there until we fulfill the demands." Lt. Hunt sighed in exasperation. "He claims if we don't come across with his demands in one hour, he's going to start killing hostages. Do you think he's the type to live up to a threat like that?"

"Yes. He's the type who might kill them even if we do cooperate."

"Christ!" Lt. Hunt arranged to meet Santillo and Weston on Lexington Avenue. "While you're on your way there," Lt. Hunt added acidly, "you might give some thought to how the hell we can get that bastard out of the tunnel without getting those hostages killed."

9

"Ramad wants the tracks green-lighted from here to the end of the line—in both directions. He wants the cops out of the stations and out of the tunnels. He wants a Boeing 707 waiting for him at the airport. He wants it fueled and carrying twenty-million dollars in gold bullion. He's going to send one of his men up from the tunnels to look over the setup at the airport, and if the guy finds one thing not to his liking, then he will notify Ramad who will start killing passengers." Lt. Hunt put down the memo he was reading and looked at the four men gathered around him. Besides Santillo and Weston there was John Adams, a lean man with gray hair and rheumy eyes, who was representing the governor. The fourth man was the mayor's elegant Mr. Kramer.

They were sitting in the N.Y.P.D. mobile communications van, that gave them radio/telephone patch-in lines to the police commissioner, the mayor, the governor, and I.R.T. central dispatch, which was in radio contact with Ramad in the subway train. The van was parked near Thirty-seventh. Pedestrians and automobile traffic flowed by them outside on Lexington Avenue, but the areas around the subway stops at Forty-second Street and Thirty-third Street were being evacuated, in case Ramad decided to come up. In the streets around each of those stops there were enough cops to make the place look like an occupied city during war time. Ambulance and fire trucks stood at various points along the streets ready to answer emergencies. And somewhere between Thirty-third and Forty-second, thirty feet under the asphalt street, the subway car waited on the dark tracks, its passengers beginning to despair of rescue.

"We've got no choice," Kramer said, "we've got to give in to their demands. The mayor won't have those people hurt."

The governor's representative merely shrugged. "It's a lot of money," he said.

"We'll foot the bill," Kramer said grimly. "We might have to cut back by firing some useless public employees—" he looked pointedly at Santillo and Weston "—but we'll make do."

The meeting dragged on a while longer, but nothing new was settled. Only forty minutes remained before Ramad's deadline arrived and he started killing people. Santillo and Weston started to get restless and got up to leave.

"Where do you two think you're going?" demanded Kramer.

"To have a look at the subway station," Santillo said.

"You'll stay right here until this hostage situation ends," Kramer declared. "I've had enough of your screw-ups. If not for you two the hakim wouldn't be in this mess."

"I'm not going to waste time asking how you figure it's our fault," Weston said. "I'll tell you this: we're leaving."

"I forbid it."

"Sit down, Kramer," Lt. Hunt commanded. Ignoring Kramer's startled look he asked his two detectives: "You think there might be a way to get at him?"

"It's worth a look."

"Okay. But don't do anything that might put those hostages in any more danger."

"We don't need a way to get at the hostages," Kramer declared. "We'll just pay the money and let Ramad go."

There was a telephone call for Kramer who replied, "Kramer here," then listened in silence for two minutes, his face growing paler by the second. At last he hung up and addressed the others:

"The city can't raise the ransom money," he said. "The banks won't lend it to us. The state doesn't have it to give."

"But the hostages...." Adams started.

"They're as good as dead," Kramer answered.

Santillo and Weston walked to the Thirty-third Street station. At the base of the roped-off stairway a cop was talking to a lean old-timer in an I.R.T. uniform.

"We're going in to have a look," Weston informed the cop.

"I'll show you the way," the I.R.T. man said.

The lights were off throughout the station, so the I.R.T. man led Santillo and Weston down a passageway and through the turnstyles by the beam of a flashlight.

The old-timer, named Grafton, paused some distance from the platform. "Sounds carry real well in the tunnel," Grafton informed them, "so if you want to say something that you do not want them to hear also, you'd better save it for later. Step real quietly too, last time a cop came down here to take a look at the tunnel he was a little noisy and drew their fire."

At the platform he turned off the light and pointed up the tracks to where the train car waited.

"Careful you don't fall off the platform," he warned the cops. "You land on that live rail and we can carry you home in an ashtray."

The car was easy to see. It was a hundred yards or so up the tracks. The emergency lights glowed faintly inside the car. The car's rooflights were all on, and they threw stark light on the tracks both in front and behind the car. Besides the problem of the lights, there was no cover to speak of, except for an occasional safety niche in the wall where a man could squeeze himself in to get out of the way of an oncoming train. Nobody could get within a hundred feet of the car in either direction without being seen.

As Weston's eyes grew accustomed to the dark, he could make out subtleties of shading he had not noticed at first, and he saw, farther up the tunnel, a large opening in the wall, like a side tunnel.

When they had walked back to the stairs, he asked the I.R.T. man what it was.

"Dead end side track," he answered. "Used to be used for track switching in the old days. The tunnels along here are full of them."

"A dead end," Santillo repeated bitterly. "We've been finding nothing but dead ends for the past two weeks!"

The two detectives walked back up to the street. It was hot, but for the first time in memory there were clouds in the sky, and they looked dark with rain. The heat wave was about to break and people could go back to acting human again.

On their way up the street Santillo and Weston passed the entrance of a movie theatre that was showing a Marilyn Monroe double bill, *Niagara* and *Seven Year Itch*. Santillo stopped in his tracks in front of the theatre.

"What's wrong?" Weston asked.

He followed Santillo's glance to a publicity photo for *Seven Year Itch*, the famous shot of Marilyn Monroe holding down her billowing skirt.

"What makes her skirt fly up like that?"

"She's standing over a...."

A metal grating in the pavement that opened down into a subway tunnel. When the train passes, air leaps up. Santillo and Weston had watched their share of legs exposed this way right here on Lexington Avenue. Above the gratings leading to the tunnel.

They went back to the subway station, and brought Grafton, the I.R.T. man, up to street level and found the nearest grating.

"The grill is really a vent for the tunnel," he told the cops, "lets 'em breathe. They'd stink to high heaven without that breathing."

"So this opens right down onto the Lex tracks?"

"Not straight down, no. Kids would be throwing all kinds of unwanted stuff down onto the track if it did—including maybe each other." He frowned in thought, adding, "I see what you're getting at. But this vent isn't near the train." He looked back at the station entrance, estimating distances, then started walking up the Avenue. In the middle of the block he stopped and again looked back to judge the distance from the station. Then he pointed straight down at the pavement, and commented: "I'd say the train was right under here."

Fifteen feet further up the sidewalk another grill stretched its crosshatchings across the sidewalk. Beneath the grill they could see nothing but darkness, but somewhere down there was the tunnel.

"Could we reach the top of the subway car from this grating?" Weston wanted to know.

"It's possible. The vents wind a funny path down sometimes, and this one might end up over the car. There's only one way to find out for sure, and that's to go down it and see."

It took ten minutes to dislodge the metal grating, and required four sturdy cops to lift it off without making enough noise to wake the dead. When the grill was off, Santillo and Weston sat down on the edge of the hole, their legs dangling in darkness, like a couple of scuba divers ready to plunge. They made sure their guns were securely holstered, then, after Weston had flicked his flashlight briefly to find footing on the concrete ledge rimming the hole, they eased themselves down.

Six feet beneath the ledge, bulky sewer and gas pipes and electrical conduits cut horizontally across the hole. Santillo and Weston lowered themselves to the pipes. The vent followed the pipes for a ways, so the two cops hunched down on hands and knees and crawled along the pipes.

"The goddamn subway car is in the other direction," Santillo observed bitterly.

Weston shrugged. There was nothing they could do about that now, they simply had to take the vent to wherever it led. Fifteen feet along, the pipes entered the wall, and the vent shaft took a downward turn. This shaft dropped ten feet to a dirt floor.

From there the vent moved horizontally again, paralleling the tracks back toward the train. The shaft was wide enough for the two men to move side by side, but the ceiling was low and they had to crawl on their bellies. After traveling a ways in pitch darkness they could see a faint glow in the floor up ahead, where a metal grating was laid across a vent opening in the ceiling of the subway tunnel.

They moved more cautiously now because any sound they made would easily carry to the tunnel. They were a dozen feet from the faint light of the grill when a dark shape appeared between them and the grill. The dark shape began to hiss. Weston flicked on the light for a second, and the cops could see that the dark shape was a huge sewer rat.

The rat was protecting a nest of half a dozen babies, and was determined not to let the two cops come closer. It reared up, hissing, its pink eyes glowing angrily.

Santillo tried to club it with his pistol, but the rat was quick: it ducked the pistol and sunk its teeth into Santillo's forearm, and hung on, yanking its head back and forth as though trying to rip Santillo's arm off. And to Santillo it felt that the rat was succeeding: fierce pain seared his forearm to the elbow. But he stifled a grunt of pain that might be heard and waited as Weston clubbed the animal to death with his .38.

"Very clever," Weston whispered, "to grab the rat's mouth with your arm and then hold it so I could kill it. Keep up the good work, Santillo."

They crawled past the nest of rats and reached the grating, which was curved to fit the arch of the tunnel ceiling. The opening was a good twelve feet in front of the subway car. They could see through the front windshield of the car into the driver's compartment where one of the Arabs stood guard. His nervous eyes scanned the tunnel floor and walls with the regularity of a radar sweep, but he never looked up at the ceiling.

Santillo and Weston started to try to lift the heavy grating, then stopped as one of the side doors of the subway car slid open and Ramad appeared. He rolled the body of a dead man onto the tracks, then paused a moment, listening, still as a nervous cat. Then he closed the door.

The two cops went back to the task of removing the grating. They had got one edge pried loose when they heard an electrical wheeze and the subway car started to move up the tracks. . . .

When Santillo and Weston were still in the middle of their confrontation with the rat in the vent, Ramad was starting to get very annoyed by the frightened faces of the passengers, the wide staring eyes. He would have liked to poke out every one of them.

"Bow your heads," he said to them. "I don't want to see your faces."

One man did not obey, a small wiry old man with a hooked nose and no fear in his eyes.

"You do not frighten me," the man declared, and Ramad could see that that was true. Ramad could not tolerate defiance of any sort: before long it spread and you were faced with insurrection. Ramad brought his gun up and placed it against the man's forehead, but still no fear entered his eyes.

"Don't shoot him," Dawn Palmer cried.

The gun bucked and the man slumped, dead. Ramad looked at the other passengers to make sure they all had learned the lesson, then he dragged the man over to the door and rolled him out and onto the track bed. During the incident the two Arabs at the back of the car did not remove their eyes from the dark track behind the train.

As Ramad started to close the door he heard a sound from somewhere in the tunnel, a faint scraping sound. It might have been nothing more than the final spasms of the dead man. It might have been something else.

His eyes raked the shadows, found nothing.

"Anyone out there?" he asked the rear guards.

"No sir."

Ramad opened the door at the front of the car and spoke to the Arab who stood guard inside.

"Anything?" he asked.

A shake of the head.

Yet something had made a noise in the tunnel. Ramad's eyes worked at the static darkness, then he came to a decision:

"Let's move the train down the tracks. Stop it just after the next station."

"Is that safe?"

"We've been here too long. In fact, to be on the safe side, from now on we should move it every ten to fifteen minutes. A moving target is harder to hit." He closed the door, and a moment later the train began to move. . . .

Santillo and Weston were frozen in surprise for a moment, then, as the subway car approached, they heaved the grating off the vent opening. They didn't worry about making noise now, they just wanted to clear the opening before the accelerating subway car passed under them. The grating clanged against the wall, and both detectives squirmed through the opening and down onto the roof of the car. There was only a couple of feet clearance, and they had to lie flat on their stomachs. The car gathered speed and, rocking back and forth, it passed through the station at Thirty-third, then went into a curve. Santillo had a good hold on the vent in the middle of the roof, but Weston was off to one side and as the train entered the curve its rocking movement sent Weston sliding toward the edge.

He tried to stop his slide with his hands, but there was nothing to grab a hold of and he could not gain a purchase on the smooth surface. He dug a toe into the roof coping, and that stopped him for a few seconds, but just then the car hit the wide part of the curve, and his foot was jarred away and again he was sliding out.

Keeping hold of the roof vent, Santillo swung his feet toward Weston, and Weston reached out, grabbed at a pantleg, missed, reached again and this time got a solid grip on his partner's leg. He held on until the train had finished the turn, then he pulled himself back to the middle of the roof. The subway car eased to a halt in the dark reaches south of the Thirty-third Street station. Further up the tunnel, the lights of the next station washed across the tracks.

The Arab in the driving compartment was of little immediate concern to Santillo and Weston because while he was inside the compartment, he presented no immediate threat to the hostages. But Ramad and the two rear guards were in the passenger area, and if Santillo and Weston were to make a move on the car they had to hit those three before they could do anybody any harm.

Santillo stuck his head out over the edge of the roof and glanced down into the train car. There was only one guard at the rear of the car. The second man had moved to the middle of the car and was keeping watch out the side window. Ramad paced up and down between the walls of frightened hostages, nervously talking to the guard at the rear, and then coming back to the other end to shout questions through the locked door to the man in the driver's compartment.

"Any sign of them?"

"No, sir," came the shout from the other side of the door.

"Well, be ready!" Like a jungle animal he sensed danger, but could not yet locate its precise source.

"Let's make our move," Weston whispered to his partner, "before he decides to move the damn train again."

Weston crawled to the rear of the car where he waited above the back door, just inches above the head of the guard there.

Santillo crawled to the place above the side doors.

Perhaps from habit rather than necessity the hostages were not sitting in front of the door, and this offered the clearest shot at the men inside.

Santillo was positioning himself over the doors, when the Arab jumped away from his post at the side window, saying, "What was that?"

The Arab came over to the doors and flung them open. Santillo lifted his head back out of the way but he was just a moment too late and the Arab shouted a warning to the others: "The roof!" He raised his gun to shoot and Santillo brought his snubnose .38 down and let the guy have it in the face. His head exploded in a geysering mist of red and gray, and he toppled backward into Ramad.

The guard at the rear started to spin around, but he only got partially turned when Weston reached down and shot the guy.

Santillo and Weston had the jump on them, and the whole thing might have been over right then, if not for the driver. He did not charge out of the driving compartment to see what was going on, he followed Ramad's instructions: he jumped on the accelerator, and the train lunged, iron wheels spinning then catching, and the subway car started to move.

With the car leaping forward the way it did, Santillo couldn't have got another shot off if he'd tried: it was all he could do to stay on the car at all, and when it hit its first curve, his weight carried him right off the roof. He managed to get a grip on the roof coping, and then swung down off the roof and straight through the open door of the car. He landed unsteadily, but immediately flung himself at Ramad who was just now getting to his feet.

Santillo dived under Ramad's rising gun, burying his head in the Arab's stomach, ramming him into the far wall. He reached up and locked his left hand on the killer's gun hand. Then the train car lurched, and the two men rolled struggling across the floor of the accelerating car. Ramad squeezed off a shot and the slug ricocheted off a handrail and shattered a window, and the passengers cowered as low to the floor as they could get.

Santillo got in a couple of hard punches with his free hand, but Ramad had a stomach like steel plating, and the blows didn't seem to effect him. He was interested only in keeping control of the gun, and getting it pointed at Santillo's head. All the while Ramad worked at that objective he was cursing Santillo in Arabic, a low grating monotone that complemented the clicketing progress of the fast-moving subway car.

Meanwhile, Weston was still on the roof. There was nothing at the back to hang onto, making it impossible to lower himself to the back door, so he started clawing his way toward the front of the car. He hugged the center of the roof and—arms and legs spread wide—he inched his way forward, while, less than a foot above his head, the unyielding concrete dome of the tunnel ceiling flew past, stirring the fine hairs at the back of his neck.

There was a headlamp in the roof above the driving compartment and Weston was able to lock one arm around it. He edged forward beyond the front end of the car, until he could just make out the figure of the Arab at the controls, a phantom figure, flashing in and out of existence under the quickly passing tunnel lamps. But the Arab got a glimpse of Weston at the same time, and for a moment the two men were looking straight into each other's eyes. Instead of going for the .45 automatic that was lying next to him on the controls, the Arab simply dropped to the floor of the car, letting up on the accelerator switch and putting on the brakes. The train wheels locked and shrieked, and the train started grinding to a halt.

By all rights, Weston's momentum should have thrown him down to the track bed, where he would have been cut in half by the locked wheels sliding on the rails. But Weston saw the Arab's intention and reacted instantly: as soon as the Arab started to drop to the floor, Weston reached up and locked both his hands tightly around the roof light. As the subway car cut speed, Weston's body was thrown straight forward, and he was left dangling across the front of the car. He put every ounce of his strength into holding on to that light, and managed to keep a grip on it until the subway train had come to a complete stop.

Inside the compartment the Arab got to his feet. His jaw dropped in surprise when he saw Weston hanging down across the front windshield, but he recovered quickly, and reached for his gun. He was already smiling in anticipation as he got the gun into his fist. Weston let go of the light and dropped to the track bed. He fell backward, his back sinking into the gravel of the road bed. He dug out his .38.

There was glare on the windshield and he could not see the Arab, but he squeezed off a shot anyway and the window quickly became a cobweb around a hole. There was a yelp from inside, and then the killer's gun flashed flame, and the windshield shattered and rocks danced around Weston's head as slugs started plowing the track bed. Weston squeezed off three quick shots at the Arab's flashing gun and there was another scream, and then the firing stopped. But it started up again a second later as the guy appeared in the shattered windshield opening, gun raised.

Weston rolled away from slugs that punched the track bed where he'd been lying, steadied himself, and shot the man in the face. The slug lifted the top right off his head, and the Arab toppled over into the darkness of the driving compartment. Weston climbed in through the broken windshield, reloaded his .38, then pushed open the door and went into the passenger area, ready to help Santillo. But Santillo wasn't around to be helped.

When the subway car started braking, Santillo and Ramad were flung violently apart, Ramad rolling to the front of the train car and Santillo caught up in the legs of a man who was clinging to a seat. The car finally shuddered to a halt and Ramad got to his feet, the silenced automatic still in his hand.

The first thing Ramad caught sight of was the hakim lying sprawled across the floor at the end of the car. It was clear that hakim Abdul Abidi had managed to escape his avengers: the hakim was lying hunched against the wall, and his neck had a right angle bend in it where no angles ought to be; his staring eyes held the emptiness of death. When Ramad's glance fell to the dead man, he went perfectly still, then rage knotted the muscles of his face into a grimace like a death rictus. He looked at Santillo and focused all of his frustrated anger on the unarmed cop.

"You're the cause of all this: If not for you I'd have Abidi out of the country by now!" He raised the gun.

Santillo saw a madman's rage in the Arab killer, the kind of rage that would not be satisfied by Santillo's death, but would spill over onto the innocent passengers trapped in this car. Santillo had a choice: die here and have Ramad turn his gun on the others, or make a run for it and try to lure Ramad after him, far enough away from the car for the hostages to disperse.

Santillo rolled across the car as Ramad's automatic jumped and a slug tunneled the floor behind him. Santillo kept on rolling right out the open door, landing awkwardly on the rail of the next track and sprawling on the track bed, bringing himself up just inches shy of the live rail. He got to his feet and ran back along the track as Ramad came to the door and fired again, this shot whining by Santillo's swinging arm and careening off the tunnel wall. Santillo started zigzagging and Ramad's next shot went way wide. On the left up ahead yawned the entrance of a side tunnel, and Santillo dived for the ground, then crawled the last few yards to the entrance. In the safety of the tunnel mouth he looked back at the train.

Ramad went back into the train, and reappeared a moment later, dragging Dawn Palmer with him. He flung her off the car, then jumped down next to her, grabbed her by the hair and hauled her to her feet. He came after Santillo while holding her as a shield. Blinded by anger, Ramad stepped carelessly over the live rail, as though it were just another obstacle instead of an immediate threat to his life.

Half of Santillo's objective was accomplished: he'd got Ramad away from the other passengers. The next half would be harder: staying alive long enough for Weston to get to him.

"Which way did they go?" Weston demanded.

But all he got from the passengers were numbed stares. They'd been doing their best to stay out of sight, they hadn't been keen to see which direction Santillo had taken.

Weston looked along the tracks: a side tunnel opened on the left and farther down the tracks a tunnel opened on the right. But no evidence of Santillo or Ramad.

Weston tried to read the signs of their movements in the gravel of the track bed, but he was no tracker, and they were just confused markings to him. He walked back along the tracks to the first side tunnel. Under the glare of overhead lights, the tracks of this tunnel disappeared around a curve to the right. He looked back at the main tracks and then he saw—or thought he saw—movement further down the line, at the mouth of the second tunnel. It could have been a rat scurrying in the shadows, but Weston had no way of knowing. He hurried down there to have a look....

Santillo had followed the first side tunnel through a long curve, and then he entered a huge high-ceilinged area, like an underground cavern. And there the tracks simply ended at the dirt wall at the far end of the cavern. There was no way out of the cavern except back the way he had come.

The cavern was littered with piles of construction materials, as though the side tunnel were soon to be extended: spools of metal cable, railway track ties, bags of concrete mix. A couple of large sheets of corrugated metal sheeting leaned on one wall, and near another wall was a stack of lumber. The only place of concealment in the tunnel was between the long stack of lumber and the wall, but that would hide him for only a few seconds: all Ramad had to do to find Santillo was to walk over to the wall and glance behind the lumber. The cavern suddenly looked like nothing as much as a grandiose grave. . . .

In his moving to look over the cave, Santillo nearly stepped on the live rail: he hadn't been thinking about it, and here on the side tracks they didn't bother to put up signs to keep reminding you. The live rail. He looked at it, and his feeling about it changed from one of fear to fascination. It was his only weapon. The question was, how could he put it to use?

He dragged a sheet of the corrugated metal over to a wall of the cavern. He positioned it on the ground near that wall so that if Ramad wanted to get a decent look behind the stack of lumber, he'd have to stand on the corrugated sheeting. Then he went over to the spool of metal cable, cut off a long piece and ran it from the sheet metal over to the tracks. He used a pair of two-by-fours to prop up the end of the cable so that it hung just inches above the live rail. One slight push and the two-by-fours would fall, and the cable would touch the live rail. Then Santillo found a small piece of four-by-four that looked good for throwing, and put it behind the lumber pile. The setup wasn't conspicuous, but it was the kind of thing that Ramad would notice, if he had time to look the room over. That meant that Santillo couldn't afford to give him that time.

Santillo positioned himself in the open near the lumber pile, where Ramad would see him as soon as he came in. Santillo wanted to get behind the lumber as soon as Ramad appeared, but he could not manage it. Ramad moved quietly as falling snow and he came around the corner so suddenly that Santillo was caught flat-footed, and Ramad got a shot off before Santillo could move. The slug hit Santillo across the back, tunneled a raw trench across his shoulder then buried itself in the cavern wall. Santillo scooted back behind the lumber as a second shot punched into the wall. Ramad threw Dawn Palmer to the ground and started to move across toward the wall so that he could look behind the stacked lumber.

"I've got you now, you bastard," he shouted triumphantly. "You mucked up my operation in this country and now you'll pay the price." He was next to the wall now, edging along it for a better look at the gap between lumber and wall where Santillo lay hidden. He was still a good ten feet short of the metal sheet.

Santillo picked up the short piece of four-by-four and got ready. The wound in his back ached when he hefted the light piece. It might effect his aim, and he knew he would have just a split-second to take aim at the end of the cable and throw this piece of wood to dislodge its support, and that if he hesitated Ramad might have time to get off a fatal shot.

From where he was hidden, Santillo could see the sheet of corrugated metal. The cable gleamed a path from the metal to the tracks, like a comet's tail, and in sudden despair Santillo did not see how Ramad could possibly miss seeing it. But Santillo underestimated Ramad's obsession with killing him: the Arab was so intensely focused on Santillo that he did not notice much of anything, and he stepped onto the corner of the metal, then took another step, and finally a third, which put him right in the center of the sheet. And now he could see Santillo.

Santillo jumped to his feet, his arm cocked to throw the four-by-four. But Dawn Palmer—who had been watching horrified—was standing directly in the line of his throw. He couldn't even see the end of the cable, let alone hit it.

Santillo leapt and tumbled over the stack of lumber, rolling down the other side of the stack and then hitting the gravel floor of the cavern and continuing to roll as a slug bit into the wood behind him sending up a shower of splinters.

Santillo couldn't risk a glance at the cable; he had to go by feel. He scrambled frantically across the ground until he thought that his angle on the cable-end had changed enough to give him a clear throw, then he came up on one knee and heaved the four-by-four with all the strength his wounded arm could muster.

It seemed to happen in slow motion. The four-by-four spinning toward its lethal destination as Ramad —pivoting to follow Santillo—raised and steadied his gun on his now stationary target. Then it occurred to Ramad to wonder what the hell Santillo was up to and instead of firing he glanced at the destination of the thrown piece of wood. He recognized the trap and made a last ditch effort to save himself. And it was that momentary letup in his pursuit of Santillo that saved the cop's life.

Ramad had time enough to take one step and then the four-by-four knocked the props out from under the cable and the cable fell onto the live rail, and carried the lethal charge of electricity across the cavern to Ramad.

The electricity surged into him with a singeing crackle and the Arab was riveted to the sheet metal. He started to shake like a man with palsy, his entire body vibrating as every muscle contracted convulsively under the electrical impulse. His locked muscles held him vertical a moment, then he collapsed slowly onto the sheet of metal and his clothes started flaming and smoke started rising into the tunnel, and the foul stench of burning flesh began to fill the cavern.

Dawn Palmer looked away in horror, then fell with relief into Santillo's arms.

Weston came running into the cavern.

"You okay?" he asked his partner.

Santillo shrugged, and winced as a flame of pain singed his shoulder. "I'll live, I guess."

"That makes two of us," Weston commented, and they stood grinning at each other for a couple of seconds.

Then, with Dawn Palmer supported between them, the two detectives started walking out of the tunnel and headed up to the street where a light rain was beginning to fall on the city.

5 EXCITING ADVENTURE SERIES MEN OF ACTION BOOKS

___NINJA MASTER
by Wade Barker
Committed to avenging injustice, Brett Wallace uses the ancient Japanese art of killing as he stalks the evildoers of the world in his mission.
___#5 BLACK MAGICIAN (C30-178, $1.95)
___#7 SKIN SWINDLE (C30-227, $1.95)
___#8 ONLY THE GOOD DIE (C30-239, $2.25, U.S.A.)
(C30-695, $2.95, Canada)

___THE HOOK
by Brad Latham
Gentleman detective, boxing legend, man-about-town, The Hook crossed 1930's America and Europe in pursuit of perpetrators of insurance fraud.
___#1 THE GILDED CANARY (C90-882, $1.95)
___#2 SIGHT UNSEEN (C90-841, $1.95)
___#5 CORPSES IN THE CELLAR (C90-985, $1.95)

___S-COM
by Steve White
High adventure with the most effective and notorious band of military mercenaries the world has known—four men and one woman with a perfect track record.
___#3 THE BATTLE IN BOTSWANA (C30-134, $1.95)
___#4 THE FIGHTING IRISH (C30-141, $1.95)
___#5 KING OF KINGSTON (C30-133, $1.95)

___BEN SLAYTON: T-MAN
by Buck Sanders
Based on actual experiences, America's most secret law-enforcement agent—the troubleshooter of the Treasury Department—combats the enemies of national security.
___#1 A CLEAR AND PRESENT DANGER (C30-020, $1.95)
___#2 STAR OF EGYPT (C30-017, $1.95)
___#3 THE TRAIL OF THE TWISTED CROSS (C30-131, $1.95)
___#5 BAYOU BRIGADE (C30-200, $1.95)

___BOXER UNIT—OSS
by Ned Cort
The elite 4-man commando unit of the Office of Strategic Studies whose dare-devil missions during World War II place them in the vanguard of the action.
___#3 OPERATION COUNTER-SCORCH (C30-128, $1.95)
___#4 TARGET NORWAY (C30-121, $1.95)

The Best of Adventure by RAMSAY THORNE

___RENEGADE #1		(C30-827, $2.25)
___RENEGADE #2	BLOOD RUNNER	(C30-780, $2.25)
___RENEGADE #3	FEAR MERCHANT	(C30-774, $2.25)
___RENEGADE #4	DEATH HUNTER	(C90-902, $1.95)
___RENEGADE #5	MACUMBA KILLER	(C30-775, $2.25)
___RENEGADE #6	PANAMA GUNNER	(C30-829, $2.25)
___RENEGADE #7	DEATH IN HIGH PLACES	(C30-776, $2.25)
___RENEGADE #8	OVER THE ANDES TO HELL	(C30-781, $2.25)
___RENEGADE #9	HELL RAIDER	(C30-777, $2.25)
___RENEGADE #10	THE GREAT GAME	(C90-737, $1.95)
___RENEGADE #11	CITADEL OF DEATH	(C30-778, $2.25)
___RENEGADE #12	THE BADLANDS BRIGADE	(C30-779, $2.25)
___RENEGADE #13	THE MAHOGANY PIRATES	(C30-123, $1.95)
___RENEGADE #14	HARVEST OF DEATH	(C30-124, $1.95)
___RENEGADE #15	TERROR TRAIL	(C30-125, $1.95)
___RENEGADE #16	MEXICAN MARAUDER	(C30-255, $2.25)
___RENEGADE #17	SLAUGHTER IN SINALOA	(C30-257, $2.25)
___RENEGADE #18	CAVERN OF DOOM	(C30-258, $2.25)

DIRTY HARRY
by DANE HARTMAN

Never before published or seen on screen.

He's "Dirty Harry" Callahan—tough, unorthodox, no-nonsense plain-clothesman extraordinaire of the San Francisco Police Department...Inspector #71 assigned to the bruising, thankless homicide detail...A consummate crimebuster nothing can stop—not even the law!

___# 1 DUEL FOR CANNONS	(C90-793, $1.95)
___# 2 DEATH ON THE DOCKS	(C90-792, $1.95)
___# 5 FAMILY SKELETONS	(C90-857, $1.95)
___# 6 CITY OF BLOOD	(C30-051, $1.95)
___# 7 MASSACRE AT RUSSIAN RIVER	(C30-052, $1.95)
___# 8 HATCHET MEN	(C30-049, $1.95)
___#10 BLOOD OF THE STRANGERS	(C30-053, $1.95)
___#11 DEATH IN THE AIR	(C90-053, $1.95)
___#12 DEALER OF DEATH	(C30-054, $1.95)

To order, use the coupon below. If you prefer to use your own stationery, please include complete title as well as book number and price. Allow 4 weeks for delivery.

WARNER BOOKS
P.O. Box 690
New York, N.Y. 10019

Please send me the books I have checked. I enclose a check or money order (not cash), plus 50¢ per order and 50¢ per copy to cover postage and handling.*

_____ Please send me your free mail order catalog. (If ordering only the catalog, include a large self-addressed, stamped envelope.)

Name _____
Address _____
City _____
State _____ Zip _____

*N.Y. State and California residents add applicable sales tax.